THE PATH TO YOU

THE JETTY BEACH SERIES BOOK 7

CLAIRE KINGSLEY

Always Have LLC

ABOUT THIS BOOK

The Path to You was originally published as Could Be the Reason: A Back to Jetty Beach Romance.

He'll protect her no matter the cost

Although I've achieved my dream of owning my own restaurant, something is still missing from my life. I'm the one guy I know who didn't get the girl.

And then Sadie walks into my life.

She works for me, so I'm not supposed to want her. But she awakens something inside me I thought was dead and gone. I was numb, and she makes me feel again.

She's running from her past, but I won't let it catch her. I'll protect her from whatever she left behind. She gave me a reason to care. If she'll let me, I'll give her a reason to trust and show her we belong together.

1

SADIE

$\mathcal{T}$he guy at table ten is making me sick to my stomach.

He's been leering at me since I took his drink order. The Porthole Inn isn't fancy, but the customers are usually nice. Lots of families, sometimes couples on dates, groups of friends. This guy? He's sitting alone and he watches me wherever I go.

I duck into the kitchen to get out of his line of sight. I wish he would just leave already. He's been taking his sweet damn time eating his top sirloin and baked potato. The way he keeps licking his lips while his eyes linger on my chest is creepy beyond words. I'm a little worried he might wait until I get off work and follow me outside.

Well, I have a can of pepper spray for a reason. I'll have it in my hand when I walk out to my car after my shift.

For now, I just need to keep doing my job. I'm new here, and the last thing I want to do is get in trouble. I barely have enough to make rent on my new place, what with having to pay the deposit, plus first and last. That wiped out what little I had saved up.

This has been a decent place to work, up until tonight. Todd, the manager, is gruff, but the tips aren't bad. I figure if I keep my head down and don't piss anyone off, I can fly under the radar and make enough money to get back on my feet. Starting over isn't easy.

I take a second to tighten my ponytail and smooth out my little black apron before I brave the dining room again. Creepy guy's eyes are on me the second I step out of the kitchen. I pointedly ignore him and go check on table twelve.

"Can I get you anything else?" I ask.

They're a cute couple—both have rings, so I'm pretty sure they're married. The woman has a mass of blond curls and a bright smile. Her husband is attractive, with pleasant green eyes and dark hair.

"I think we're fine," the woman says.

"No dessert, sunshine?" the man asks.

"I'm so full," she says. "Maybe next time."

"No problem," I say and slide the black folder with the bill onto the table. "Whenever you're ready. No rush."

I don't want to check on creepy guy again, but I need to take table nine's order, and that's right next to him. I keep my eyes forward as I walk by his table, and stand so his back is to me. He actually turns around in his seat to watch me. I fidget and try to focus on writing down table nine's orders.

Deep breaths, Sadie. He can't do anything. He can look, and his thinly veiled sexual innuendo is disgusting, but soon he'll be gone and I won't have to deal with him anymore. I've got this.

I slip my notepad into my apron pocket and head toward the back. I've barely taken two steps when I feel a hand on my wrist, the grip like a vise.

"Let go of me," I say, hissing under my breath.

Creepy guy's lip turns up in a horrifying approximation of a smile. He's right on the edge of his seat, his hand clamped down on my wrist.

"Come here, sugar," he says.

Fear and rage surge through me and flashes of memory race through my mind. I'm pinned down, unable to move. Helpless. I gasp and try to blink the images away. My heart speeds up and adrenaline courses through my system.

"Let go." I think it's my voice, but I feel like I'm no longer in control of my body. I'm floating above myself, watching this scene play out as if it's happening to someone else.

"Come on, sugar, be nice." He tugs on my arm, hard, and I stumble toward him.

The detached feeling intensifies. I'm completely numb. I watch as my other hand balls into a fist and flies toward his face. There should probably be pain, but I feel nothing as my knuckles smack into his nose. He lets go of my wrist and I jerk backward.

Noise comes back to me in a rush, as if I was momentarily deaf. The guy howling in pain as he clutches his face, blood leaking out beneath his hands. The startled exclamations of the other customers. Todd's angry voice, demanding to know what's going on.

I bolt into the kitchen. Oh my god. What did I just do? Did I hit him? I look down at my hand. My knuckles are red and I can still feel the sensation of his nose crunching. Holy shit, I think I broke it. My hand aches, and my other wrist burns where he held me. I have red marks in the shape of his fingers.

The cooks stare at me, and within seconds, the rest of the staff is talking in whispers, casting wary glances my direction.

Todd marches back into the kitchen, his face full of fury. "Sadie. My office. Now."

I swallow hard and follow him back, still reeling from shock. He closes the door behind me. I have a momentary flight reaction that's so strong, I almost run out to my car.

"You're fired," he says. Nothing else. He doesn't ask me what happened, nor does he appear to care. That's it. I'm out the door.

"Todd, he—"

"You just broke a customer's nose," he says. "We could be sued over this."

I hold up my wrist, still red where he grabbed me. "He held my arm and wouldn't let go."

He eyes my wrist for half a second. "Still. You hit him. I can't promise he's not going to call the police."

My shoulders slump. You have to be kidding me. I must have a big *fuck with me, no one will care* sign on my back. Apparently jackass men can do whatever they want to me, and the minute I try to stand up for myself, I'm the one who gets screwed.

I moved to this stupid town thinking I could get away from this bullshit. But I suppose it exists everywhere.

"I'm not sorry that I hit that jerk." I'm either going to lash out in anger, or crumple to the ground and cry. Anger it is. "He was staring at me and making disgusting comments all night, and his hand on me was the last straw. So fuck you, Todd."

I whirl around and fly out of his office. I grab my coat and purse and stomp my way out of the kitchen to the back door. Pausing before I go into the parking lot, I get out my pepper spray. If that dick is out there waiting for me, I'm going to blind his sorry ass. I can feel fear trying to take hold, so I grasp onto the rage pouring through me like a lifeline. I can fall apart at home. I have to at least get to my car. Anger keeps me afloat.

My hands shake and I have a feeling if I *am* attacked, I won't be able to use the stupid pepper spray. Tears fall down my cheeks—tears of impotent anger and frustration. Memories swirl through my brain, the old ones mingling with the new. It's hard to keep them separate.

I pause next to my car and take a few shaking breaths. Keys. I need my keys. I slip the pepper spray into my pocket and pull my keys out of my purse.

"Excuse me?"

The woman's voice makes me jump—literally. I clutch my chest and turn around, breathing hard.

"I am *so* sorry," she says. It's the woman with the curly blond hair from table twelve. Her husband is next to her, concern in his eyes. "Are you okay?"

"Yes," I say, but my voice trembles. I wish she'd just let me go. I'm holding on by such a thin thread, and the sympathy in her voice almost breaks me.

"Can I see your hand?" the man asks. "I'm a doctor."

I glance down at my knuckles. They're red and starting to swell. "I think I'm fine."

"Maybe, but I'd feel better if you'd let me take a quick look." He steps forward. "I'm Cody Jacobsen. This is my wife, Clover."

I swallow hard. "Sadie Sedgwick."

"It's nice to meet you, Sadie," Clover says, nothing but sincerity in her voice. "Are you new in town?"

"Yes."

I hold out my hand and Cody looks it over. "It doesn't look broken. Can I touch it?"

I wonder if he has any idea how grateful I am that he asked first before touching me. "Sure."

He places his palm beneath mine to keep it steady and gently probes the back of my hand. "Can you move your fingers for me?"

I wiggle my fingers. It hurts a little, but not too much.

"Good," he says. "I don't think you need an x-ray. Ice it when you get home to ease any swelling. If it swells up a lot, or you find you're having trouble moving your fingers, get it checked out, okay?" He pulls out his wallet and hands me a business card. "My clinic is open seven days a week."

I take the card and tuck it in my purse. "Thank you. I think I'll be okay."

"What happened in there was horrible," Clover says. "You were a badass."

Cody laughs. "Clover."

"She was. You saw how he grabbed her. He needed a good punch in the nose."

"Well, my boss didn't think so." I close my mouth quickly. I shouldn't be dumping on these people. They've been very nice, but they don't need to hear about my problems.

"What?" Clover asks. "What happened?"

"It's nothing," I say. "I'm sorry. I have to get home."

"Wait," Clover says. "You didn't just lose your job, did you?"

"Obviously," I say. "I punched a customer."

Clover gasps, her eyes widening. "Oh my god, Cody. I told you I felt the tingle when I saw her."

"Actually, you did say that," Cody says.

"I'm sorry, I don't understand," I say.

"You're a waitress," Clover says, as if that explains everything.

"I was until a few minutes ago."

"Exactly," she says brightly. "This is perfect. I have a new job for you."

"Um, sunshine, are you sure?" Cody asks.

She gives him a rather cute eyeroll. "Yes. Positive. We need a new server. We've needed someone for weeks. This is why Gabe hasn't hired anyone yet. I was supposed to meet Sadie tonight and offer her a job. It's fate."

I'm so confused, I just stare at her. "I... what?"

Clover smiles. "I work at the Ocean Mark. It's about twenty minutes north of here, so it's a little bit of a drive. But it's so much nicer than this place." She turns to Cody. "And clearly we're never eating here again, after they fired Sadie."

"Clearly," Cody says.

Clover turns back to me. "Come in tomorrow at three. It won't be too busy on a Sunday, and Sam can start training you."

I stare at her, feeling such a mix of surprise and disbelief, I'm not even sure where I am. "I don't... Um... Okay?"

Cody gives me a reassuring smile. "It's okay, she does that to people."

"I do what to people?" she asks.

"Bewilder them."

"I do not," she says. "Anyway, tomorrow. Three. Meet me there and I'll show you around." She winks at Cody. "See? Fate!"

"Make sure you ice your hand," Cody says. "And I hope the rest of your night is better."

"Thank you," I say.

"Good night, Sadie," Clover says, beaming at me. "I'll see you at work tomorrow."

Cody shakes his head with a smile as he puts his arm around his wife. Clover waves. I stand outside my car and watch them go, not sure what just happened.

I get in my car and lock the doors. Was that real? If I show up tomorrow, am I going to discover this was some kind of prank? Or that Clover is a crazy person? She didn't seem crazy, just... enthusiastic. And Cody legitimately seemed to be a doctor, unless his business cards are fake.

How paranoid am I that I'm concocting a story about Cody and Clover that has them as con artists, posing as a doctor and his spunky wife who works in a restaurant?

I clutch the steering wheel and release a long breath. I suppose I'll go to the Ocean Mark tomorrow at three. If Clover *is* crazy, I'll just pretend like I'm lost. And if she isn't, and she really did just give me a job minutes after I got fired, I'll count my blessings.

Goodness knows this girl could use a break.

2

GABE

*M*y staff is already getting things prepped for tonight's service when I come out of my office. They're a good bunch—hard-working and professional. My kitchen has to operate like a well-oiled machine to give guests the culinary experience they've come to expect from my restaurant. I set the tone, but we have to be more than the sum of our parts. I've been fortunate to find some great people that I can count on.

Soft music plays in the background while we work. It's a Sunday, and we're not booked up, so I don't anticipate a busy night. We're in the middle of the tourist season, but Jetty Beach tends to have a lot of weekend visitors, so Sunday nights are quiet. Last night was a madhouse, so I'm sure we'll all be glad for a slight reprieve.

The first orders come in, and I'm lost in my work, hardly paying attention to what's going on around me. I work side by side with my sous chef, Clover. We've worked together for several years now, so we settle into a comfortable routine without much need for chit chat. We get the first meals plated and ready for the servers to take out.

I look up and notice someone I don't recognize. Before I can wonder what a strange woman is doing in my kitchen, our eyes meet. The air around me seems to spark and I swallow hard. Her auburn hair is pulled up and the most dazzling green eyes I've ever seen stare back at me. She has a dusting of freckles across her delicate nose and cheeks. She starts to give me a shy smile, but it fades as I watch her. Sam, one of my head servers, leans in and says something to her. They grab the plated meals and walk back to the dining room.

"Clover, who was that?"

Clover glances at me. "Who was what?"

"The woman with Sam who just took table four's dinner?"

"Oh, that's Sadie," she says with her signature smile. "She's new."

"New? I don't remember hiring anyone."

"You didn't," she says.

"Then why do we have a new server?"

"I hired her," she says.

"You what?"

Clover takes a deep breath. "I hired her. That's what restaurants do when they're short on wait staff. They hire someone."

"No, *I* hire someone when we're short on wait staff."

"Except you haven't," she says. "We've been short-staffed for weeks. Besides, it was fate. You expect me to argue with fate?"

"Oh boy," I say. Clover has this weird thing with listening to fate. "Does she have any experience?"

"Yes," Clover says brightly. "She was working at the Port-hole Inn but she got fired."

"What? You hired a server who got fired from her last

job? Clover—"

"Wait, you need to hear the whole story," she says. "It wasn't her fault. Some guy was being a jerk and he grabbed her. And then *she* got in trouble for it. It was ridiculous. But also perfect, because I was there to hire her so she could work here. It was totally meant to be."

I stare at Clover for a few seconds. I'm sure that train of logic makes perfect sense to her. But she can't just hire someone without telling me. I do the hiring around here. "Clover, I know you were just trying to help, but—"

Sadie comes back in the kitchen and I stop talking. Sam takes her over to the prep station. Apparently Clover already has Sam training her. That's... well, it's efficient, I'll give them that. Sadie meets my eyes again. They're huge and pleading with me, as if she knows she wasn't hired under normal circumstances.

Clover sidles up to me and nudges me with her elbow. "Besides, isn't she cute?"

"What?"

"She's cute, right?"

I tear my eyes away from Sadie. She's not just cute. She's beautiful. "That's beside the point. You can't hire people without telling me."

"I didn't," she says. "I just told you. And why is that beside the point?"

"It doesn't matter whether I think a server who *works for me*," I say, emphasizing the words, "is cute."

"Good, then I'm glad we agree," Clover says.

"Agree on what?"

"That she works for you," she says.

"What?"

"She is cute, though. Even you have to admit that. But we

can't stand here talking in the middle of a service. We're getting behind. Come on, chef."

I gape at Clover, wondering what the hell just happened. Sadie comes back into the kitchen with Sam. I guess we do need another server. Although if she can't hack it, I'll have to be the bad guy and let her go.

She glances at me with that same worried expression in her eyes. I look away and get back to work. She'll either sink or swim.

Although it's odd how quickly I feel a little spark of hope that she does indeed swim.

I keep my back to her and focus on the meat I'm searing. Beautiful or not, she's just another server. The last thing I need is to get caught staring at my new employee. I'll have to talk to Clover again later about not hiring people without my permission.

Dinner service goes by without any issues. The last guests leave, the door is locked, and we get things cleaned and prepped for tomorrow.

I finish wiping down the last counter when I notice Sadie shouldering a handbag. She pauses and meets my eyes.

Clover appears out of nowhere, shaking out her curls with her hand. "Oh, good. You guys met. Officially, I mean."

Sadie blinks. "Oh, not exactly."

Clover sighs, and I can tell her exasperation is meant entirely for me. "Gabe, this is our new server, Sadie. Sadie, Gabriel Parker. Geez, Gabe, I thought you would have done this earlier."

"Earlier? Clover..." I stop because sometimes reasoning with Clover is an exercise in futility. "Did you get Sadie's paperwork squared away?"

"Of course," Clover says. "And I have her mirroring Sam's schedule so he can keep training her."

"All right," I say.

"Night, chef," Clover says with a smile. "Night, Sadie. Awesome job tonight. You did great." She looks at me with raised eyebrows, like she expects me to say something.

"Yeah, thanks, Sadie."

Sadie's eyes dart between the two of us a few times. "Thanks for the opportunity. This came at the perfect time. I really appreciate it."

I look down. Those green eyes are stirring something inside of me. I'm afraid if I keep looking at her, I won't be able to stop staring.

"It was fate," Clover says, matter-of-fact.

"Sure," Sadie says, her voice echoing the skepticism I feel. "Good night."

Sadie leaves, but Clover hesitates beside me, her hands on her hips.

"What?" I ask.

"What's up with you?" she asks.

"Nothing." I head for my office but I hear Clover's footsteps behind me.

She follows me in. "I'm texting Cody to tell him I'll be late."

"Why? We're finished early. You can go home." I take off my chef coat while Clover types. I don't bother waiting for her to leave before I pull off my t-shirt. I learned a long time ago that Clover doesn't have the same sense of propriety that most people have. And since she's married to my sister's brother-in-law, she considers me more of a brother than a boss. Which, in Clover-land, apparently means I can change my shirt in front of her and it's not weird.

"Because we're going out," she says. "You need a drink."

I put on a fresh t-shirt. "Do I?"

"Clearly," she says. "Come on. I'll buy."

MY FRIEND FINN'S IRISH PUB is mostly empty. A small group sits at a table and there are a couple people sitting at the bar. Clover picks a table and hangs her coat over the back of her chair.

Finn comes over, wiping his hands on a white towel. "Bourbon?"

"That works," I say.

He turns to Clover and hesitates. "Normally I'd say Corona with lime, but somehow that seems wrong. What can I get you?"

She smiles at Finn. "Just a club soda with lemon."

"You got it," he says.

"Okay, grumpy man," Clover says as soon as Finn is out of earshot. "What's going on?"

"Grumpy?" I ask. "I'm not grumpy."

She raises her eyebrows. "Well, you're always a little broody. But it seems like something is going on with you lately."

Finn brings our drinks and I take a sip of my bourbon. It slides down my throat, leaving a trail of warmth. I stare at the table for a long moment, then take another drink. But I still don't answer Clover's question.

"Fine, if you don't want to talk about you, let's talk about the menu," she says. "It's been eight months since we changed anything. Don't you think it's time?"

It is time. Well past it. But talking about the menu is touching on all the things I don't want to think about—let alone talk about. But I should say *something*.

"We do need to switch out a few menu items. We'll keep some of our mainstays. Maybe we can just go back to last year's entrees."

"That's... interesting," she says. "Don't you think we can come up with some new ideas?"

New ideas. How do I tell her I'm out of ideas? That I haven't had a decent, fresh concept for the menu in a year? And somehow, I can't seem to make myself care.

"Maybe you should work on that," I say. "You like to experiment."

Clover opens her mouth like she's going to say something, but closes it. She twirls a curl around one finger and looks away.

This isn't like Clover. Normally she just says what's on her mind, no matter what it is. This pensive thing she's doing is odd.

"What's up?" I ask. Then it hits me. I bet she got another job. I have her working some of my off nights, leading the kitchen, which is a step up for her. But she's talented; I won't get to keep her forever. My heart squeezes a little at the thought of losing her. I know, deep down, she's the main reason my restaurant hasn't suffered. She brings her fresh ideas and her constant enthusiasm to my kitchen. Without that, I don't know where we'd be.

I don't know where I'd be.

"Well, I kind of have something to talk to you about." She runs her finger around the rim of her glass.

"It's okay," I say. "I knew I'd lose you eventually. Where are you going?"

"Lose me?" she asks. "Gabe, it will only be temporary. Are you saying I can't come back?"

"Temporary?" I ask. "Why would you come back if you got a head chef position somewhere else?"

She stares at me for a second before her face breaks in a wide smile. "Head chef? No, I didn't get another job. I'm going to need maternity leave. I'm pregnant."

I raise my eyebrows in surprise. "Pregnant? Clover, that's great. Congratulations. Of course we'll work it out."

She smiles that huge smile of hers, but there's an odd sinking feeling in my gut. Obviously I'm happy for her. Clover is family. And this shouldn't be a surprise. The Jacobsen clan has practically exploded with babies over the last couple of years. Ryan and Nicole's daughter Madeline is a toddler now, running around and starting to talk. My sister and her husband Hunter had a baby boy, Sebastian; he turned one a few months ago. Melissa and Jackson aren't actually Jacobsens, but blood relationships have never mattered much to that family; their little girl Skylar is three and Melissa is pregnant again. I'm actually surprised Cody and Clover haven't started a family before now. They've been married for a couple years.

And that's the thing. I've been inundated with weddings and babies. And they're all people I love and care about, so it should be great.

"Thanks," she says. "I've been a little nervous to tell you."

"You shouldn't have been. I'm happy for you."

She pushes my drink closer to me. "Pound that and then tell me what's going on, though. Because there's something and I'm not leaving until I know what it is."

I toss back the rest of my drink. "I don't know if I want to talk about this."

"Listen, we're not at work. I'm basically your sister. So you can tell me stuff."

Whether it's Clover's knack for getting what she wants, or the bourbon starting to do its thing, I find myself letting it all out. "Everyone around me is moving on with their lives. Do you know how many weddings I've been to in the last few years? Ryan and Nicole... Melissa's huge thing up in Seattle a few years ago... yours... my sister's... Now my two best friends are engaged. I have to be a groomsman again. Twice."

"Aw," Clover says. "It's like always being a bridesmaid, except groomsman."

"Something like that," I say. "I feel like I had my shot, you know? I *was* married, but it didn't work. She didn't want the life I did, so she left. And now all the people around me are starting their lives—starting families. And what am I doing? Working too much. I don't know what that's going to get me, besides a drinking problem." I signal to Finn for another bourbon.

"Just because your first marriage didn't work out, doesn't mean you're doomed to be alone," Clover says, her voice gentle.

"That's easy for you to say. You don't know what it's like," I say.

"What?"

"To be the one guy who *didn't* get the girl."

Clover reaches across the table and gives my hand a sympathetic squeeze.

In a way, I'm the guy who hasn't *wanted* to get the girl. At least not in the last few years. It's not like I haven't had opportunities. I've been divorced for years, and I've dated. But none of those relationships ever went anywhere, and I kind of stopped trying.

"Oh, Gabriel," Clover says. "I just know fate has something in store for you. You're one of the best guys I know."

"Don't inflate his ego too much," Finn says as he slides me another drink.

The door opens and my friend Lucas saunters in. He notices us and does a fake hat tip as he approaches our table.

"Hey, assholes," he says. "And Clover."

"You can have my seat, Lucas. I should get home." Clover stands and pats my arm. "I'll see you later."

Lucas sits down and Finn reappears with two beers. He hands one to Lucas and takes an empty chair.

"Aren't you still working?" I ask.

Finn shrugs. "It's dead in here. I doubt I'll have any more customers."

"Fair enough." I take another sip of my bourbon.

"Is it just me, or does this girls' weekend thing suck?" Lucas asks.

"What girls' weekend thing?" I ask.

"Juliet and Becca went out of town with a friend and they aren't coming home until tomorrow," Finn says.

"Why does that suck?" I ask.

"I miss my girl," Lucas says with a shrug.

This makes me sound like a dick, but life was easier when Finn and Lucas were still single. There was a sense of brotherhood; we were three guys who were in the same place in life. In one way or another, we'd all sworn off relationships. Finn wasn't opposed to meeting someone, but he'd decided he'd never get married. Personally, I thought he was smart. And then he met Juliet, and within months, he'd changed his tune. Now his wedding is a couple of months away. Lucas was happy with casual sex and no ties to anyone—until he met Becca. I can admit, Becca's a sweetheart; Lucas didn't stand a chance with her. I wasn't the least bit surprised when he told me a few weeks ago that he'd bought a ring. Then last weekend, they came back from surfing and she's wearing it. The two of them are disgustingly happy all the time. Just like Finn and Juliet.

"He's grumpy again," Lucas says, jerking his thumb at me.

"Fuck off," I say. "I'm not grumpy. Why does everyone keep saying that?"

"We need to get him laid," Lucas says. "Or at least do something fun. What about an early bachelor party? We'll get wasted, watch strippers—"

"I already told you, no strippers," Finn says.

"You really won't let me get strippers for your bachelor party?" Lucas asks.

"Will you let me get strippers for *your* bachelor party?" Finn asks.

"Fuck no," Lucas says. "Becca would hate that."

Finn stares at him with an open mouth, his beer lifted halfway.

"You realize you're a huge hypocrite, don't you?" I ask.

"Yeah, so?" Lucas asks.

"How is having strippers at *his* bachelor party any different than having them at *yours*?" I ask, but I wave my hand to brush off the question. "Never mind. It doesn't matter. I don't need strippers. Or to get drunk with you assholes."

"Well, you need something," Lucas says.

I take another sip of my drink. He's right. I do need something. I need a reason to fucking *care*. But I have no idea what that should be.

3

GABE

"You're not supposed to be here."

I breathe out a long sigh when I hear the voice. Linda, my business manager, stands in the doorway of my office. I look up from my desk. "I'm just following up on a few things."

"It's your day off," she says. Her dark hair is peppered with gray and she keeps it short in a pixie cut. She raises her eyebrows at me and puts her hands on her hips. "You told me to chase you out of here on your days off."

"Actually, I think Clover and my sister are the ones who told you that." I turn my attention back to my laptop.

"Fair enough," she says. "But they're right, you know."

"Probably."

"Well, since you're here…" She walks in and sits in one of the chairs on the other side of the desk. "The people from *Simple Pleasures* will be here in a few weeks. I just want to make sure it's on your radar now so you don't get bent out of shape when they show up."

I pinch the bridge of my nose. *Simple Pleasures* is a national lifestyle magazine and website. They did a short feature on me a while back, and came back to us recently, wanting to do a more in-depth story. "Tell me again why this is a good idea?"

"Gabe, you can't buy this kind of publicity," she says. "Remember how much business we got last time? And that was a short piece. They want to do something much bigger. The attention you get from this could easily double our business."

I do remember how much business we got. I also remember what it was like to be scrutinized, questioned, prodded, and photographed. It wasn't a pleasant experience for me. I wanted them to focus on the food, and they wanted to focus on me. I had to deflect numerous uncomfortable questions about my personal life.

Of course, Linda is right; it *will* be good for business. But that doesn't mean I have to like it.

"Fine," I say. "I'll be cooperative. But I'm not answering their questions about my relationship status."

"You know they're going to ask," she says. "You're an attractive, successful, *single* man. Their readers will want to know what's up."

"What's up is that I'm a chef," I say. "That's all they need to know."

Linda sighs. "Just be cooperative. And try to be... pleasant."

"I can be pleasant," I say.

"I know you *can*," she says. "Whether you *will* is another issue. Now get out of here. Enjoy your day off."

I smile and close my laptop. "All right, I'll go. Have a good night."

"You too," she says.

I swing by the store and pick up a few things before heading home. As usual, my house is quiet and dark. Aside from the brief time my sister Emma stayed with me when she first moved back to Jetty Beach, I've lived alone since my ex-wife Amanda left.

Every once in a while, I think about selling the house. Over time, I've gotten rid of most of the things Amanda didn't take. But the house itself is a stark reminder of what I once had, and what I lost.

However, I'm not home very much. Whenever I consider the work it would take to sell the house, then pack up and move, I usually just pour a drink and push the thought aside.

I set the groceries on the counter and pull things out of the bags. Coming up with new ideas for the menu used to be my favorite part of being a chef. When I first took over the restaurant, I'd experiment at home, in this very kitchen. New flavors. New textures. New combinations. I was all about pushing boundaries, and finding ways to excite the taste buds.

Amanda was always my first taster. She had an excellent palate and good instincts—plus enough honesty to tell me when something didn't work.

And she loved my cooking. I met her when I first moved back to the States after going to school in Europe. Even though I was working insane hours, apprenticing under an absolute tyrant of a chef, I still loved cooking for her at home. So much of our relationship revolved around food. Shopping together, cooking together, eating together. Even though I devoted an enormous amount of time to my career, she was always supportive.

Until my career went in a direction she didn't like.

She saw herself as the wife of a prominent chef in an exciting place like New York or Los Angeles. So when I got the opportunity to return to my hometown and take over the Ocean Mark, she thought I was crazy. That wasn't what an up and coming chef was supposed to do. She wanted me to carve out a place for myself somewhere trendy and important.

But my dream was always to come back here and breathe new life into the Ocean Mark. I love that place. It sits on a bluff overlooking the Pacific Ocean. Huge floor-to-ceiling windows give guests an incredible view, and a spotlight illuminates the beach after dark. The building is lodge style, with heavy wood beams, warm tones, and soft lighting that feels both luxurious and cozy. The art and décor pays homage to the Native Americans who once lived in this region. I even work with local artists to give them a place to showcase and sell their work.

That was always the life I wanted. To enjoy the slower pace in Jetty Beach, and have the best fine dining establishment on the coast.

It wasn't the life Amanda wanted. To her credit, she tried. She stuck it out for a while. But she hated small town living. It was never enough for her, and ultimately, I wasn't enough to keep her here.

After she left, I dove into my work. It was what kept me sane in those early days. I practically lived at the restaurant. But my creativity was through the roof. I was hyper-focused on cooking, on creating, on pushing boundaries and exploring ideas. For a while, it seemed as if Amanda leaving had been the best thing that could have happened to me. Without the distractions of a failing marriage, I was able to put all my energy into my restaurant. And it thrived.

But burn-out is a real thing, and after a while, my passion waned. Those flashes of inspiration that would wake me before the sun came up started to disappear. Life became routine.

And I know my cooking has suffered.

When *Simple Pleasures* did their first piece on me, I was terrified the entire time that they would see through me. They came looking for a young, talented chef who was doing exciting things with local foods and flavors. I did my best to be that man while they were here. To give them what they expected.

The truth was, I was a man struggling to find joy in food the way I once did. A man whose passion for cooking had diminished. The rest of my staff were carrying me—their creativity and enthusiasm kept my restaurant from slipping.

I'm still that man. In fact, if anything, I've fallen deeper down the hole of indifference. Instead of feeling inspired, I spend most of my time feeling numb. I go through the motions, but I have yet to figure out how to recapture what I lost.

And I know, deep down, it's only a matter of time before I'm found out. Before everyone sees the truth about who I've become. Which is why shining the light of media attention on me is the last thing I want right now.

I sharpen a knife and get to work chopping and slicing. Clearing my mind, I try to focus on the food and nothing else. I cut, stir, and sauté, smelling and tasting as I go. I have chicken breast, mushrooms, white wine—things I've used before. But maybe I can come up with a new twist on an old favorite.

After trying a few variations, I plate my creation. I'm not crazy about how it looks, but if the flavor is good, I can work on improving the presentation.

I cut a bite and taste it, pushing it around my mouth, considering. It tastes like... nothing.

It has flavor. But there's nothing interesting. Nothing exciting. It's as if the empty space inside me keeps growing, eating way at my creativity—at my passion. And everything I cook is bland.

Lately, all my food tastes like this. Most people would probably say it's fine. But fine isn't the goal. Fine is where a chef's career goes to die.

I dump the rest in the trash. Once upon a time I would have immediately started over—tried again, tweaking the spices or the cooking time. But tonight's little failure leaves me feeling spent. I clean up the dishes and pour myself a glass of wine, wondering what the hell I'm going to do to get myself back on track.

4

SADIE

*M*y feet are killing me.

I kick off my shoes and sling my purse over the back of a chair. Working as a server in a nice restaurant has its perks—the tips are fantastic—but any job that keeps you on your feet for eight hours is exhausting.

Tonight was the busiest night since I started working at the Ocean Mark. I feel like I've picked things up quickly, and I held my own. Even in the middle of the service, when it felt like I had a hundred things to remember all at once, I handled it. My tables were happy, they complimented the food, and tipped well. All in all, a good night.

Except for Gabriel, the head chef.

I'm convinced he doesn't like me. I don't know if I've done something to irritate him, or if he's still mad that Clover hired me. Either way, I've spent the last couple of weeks feeling like I'm going to wilt under his gaze.

It's not that he glares at me, exactly. He doesn't seem angry. The first time he saw me, his brow furrowed and he looked more confused than mad.

Since then, he's only spoken to me with short, gruff responses. And he still does that brow furrow thing, watching me like he's not sure what to think. I'm not sure what to think either.

The fact that he's drop-dead gorgeous is not making this situation easier. He's younger than I imagined he'd be, considering Clover told me he owns the place. He has tousled dark blond hair and piercing blue eyes that are stunning. And that brooding look he gets makes my heart race.

So now I work for a guy who doesn't seem to like me, and I practically have a crush on him. Great, Sadie. Just great.

I toss my keys on the counter and glance at the few pieces of mail sitting there. All with my name. Maybe I need to change it. I don't know if I'll ever feel completely safe, but not having Sadie Sedgwick attached to everything might help. The guy who rented me this house assured me my information is confidential. But I had to set up utilities in my name—which could be traceable. Granted, Adam would have to narrow it down to this small town, so many thousands of miles from where I started. And that isn't likely.

When I left Missouri, I could have gone anywhere, in any direction. I made sure no one knew where I was headed —or even that I was leaving at all. I sold my car, got rid of my phone. I paid cash for my bus ticket so there wouldn't be a record of me. He shouldn't be able to find me.

It all sounds so dramatic. It's still hard to believe this is what my life has become. I'm basically in hiding, although the authorities won't help me. No one will. It's hard to get help when people don't believe you.

I flop down on the couch and put my tired feet up. I can't think about Adam Cooper right now. He's far away and I have to believe he won't find me. I'll go crazy if I think about it all the time. I've done what I can to protect myself. I just have to hope it's enough.

Besides, I have more immediate concerns. Like how to get Gabriel Parker out of my head.

I flip on the TV to zone out for a while, but it isn't long before my eyes are heavy. I do a once-over on the locks on my doors and windows—like I do every single night. I know they're locked. They always are. But I won't be able to sleep unless I check.

I GET up in the morning feeling refreshed with feet that no longer ache. Since I don't have to work until three, I figure I should get some errands done, and head into town.

There's a little diner right near where I'm parked, so I decide to pop in for a late breakfast. It looks like one of those old-fashioned burger joints with a black and white checked floor and a big juke box in the corner. There's a long counter with round barstools, and booths along the window. I hear sounds coming from the kitchen, but there's no one up front. I'm not sure if this is a seat-yourself kind of place, or if I'm supposed to order at the counter. There's a stack of menus near the cash register, so I grab one and take a look.

The hair on the back of my neck stands up and I have the distinct sensation that someone's watching me. My back tingles and a little swirl of fear swims through my belly. My body stiffens and I'm about ready to leave—because something feels off—when a woman comes out from the kitchen and gives me a warm smile.

"Be right with you, sweetie," she says.

She takes a glass carafe of coffee past the booths, refilling mugs and asking if anyone needs anything. She gets to the booth at the end and the man pushes his cup toward her. His eyes lift and meet mine.

It's Gabriel.

We both freeze, like a couple of startled animals. His brow furrows and he turns away, nodding to the waitress. He slides his coffee back across the table and doesn't meet my eyes again.

This is awkward. I almost turn to go, but the waitress comes back and shows me to a table. Naturally, it's right next to Gabriel.

I sit in the booth so my back is to him, but knowing he's right there is so uncomfortable. Is he looking at me? Is he annoyed that I'm here? Why did he look at me like that? The waitress gets me coffee and hands me a menu. I really wish I'd chosen somewhere else to eat.

"Hi." Gabriel's voice startles me. I was so intent on the menu—not that I was processing anything that's on it—I didn't realize he'd approached my booth.

"Hi."

"Sorry, I didn't mean to surprise you," he says. "I just figured it was weird to sit there and pretend I don't know you. So... good morning."

"Good morning."

The waitress comes back with a plate of hash browns, eggs, bacon, and toast. "Oh, you moving tables, honey?" She plunks the plate down across from me. "Here you go. I'll get your coffee."

Gabriel's eyebrows lift and his mouth opens as he watches the waitress move his coffee to my table. He looks around, like he's trying to decide what to do.

I think I'm going to die of awkwardness if he takes his

breakfast back to his table. I tuck my hair behind my ear. "Maybe you should just have a seat. You can tell me what's good here."

"If you don't mind," he says.

"No, not at all."

He sits across from me and his mouth turns up in a small smile. His whole face changes—the severity of his expression softens and his eyes are bright. It looks more natural on him than I would have guessed. Up until now, I've only seen him scowl.

There's a little tingle in my belly at the thought that he's showing *me* that smile. Like it's a secret he doesn't share with just anyone.

"Listen, Sadie, I think maybe we got off on the wrong foot," he says. "Clover didn't give me a heads-up that she'd hired you, so it took me by surprise. That wasn't your fault."

"I was afraid of that," I say. "I'm sorry—"

He holds up a hand. "You don't have anything to apologize for. Clover kind of lives by her own rules. I've known her long enough, I shouldn't let that surprise me. And it looks like things worked out for everyone. You've been doing a great job."

His soft voice and subtle confidence puts me at ease, uncoiling the tension in my shoulders. "Well, thanks for the opportunity. It couldn't have come at a better time."

"Clover has a knack for that," he says.

I pick up the menu. "What do you suggest for breakfast? Yours looks good."

He picks up his fork and starts mixing in his eggs with his hash browns. "Yeah, you can't go wrong, if you like greasy diner food." He leans in and lowers his voice. "But don't get the sausage gravy."

The waitress comes back, coffee carafe still in hand. "Decided yet, sweetie?"

"I'll have what he's having," I say.

"Coming right up," she says.

Gabriel sprinkles a light dusting of salt and pepper over his breakfast while I stir some cream in my coffee.

"Do you eat here a lot?" I ask. "I'm kind of surprised to see you in a place like this."

He sets the pepper on the table. Is it just me, or does he look a little flushed?

"Yeah, the food here is actually pretty bad," he says. "These hash browns are made from dehydrated potatoes and the oil they use is awful."

"But you're here?" I ask.

He gives me that little smile again—the one that hints at something beneath the surface. "Yeah, I know. It's my guilty pleasure. I grew up eating here as a kid, so sometimes I come on my days off. I kind of try not to be seen."

"Oh man, I blew your cover," I say.

"That's all right." He meets my eyes. "It can be our secret."

I feel another little flutter in my tummy, but the waitress reappears with the coffee again. "Your breakfast will be out in just a minute."

"Thanks," I say.

We sip our coffee in silence, but the quiet is comfortable, rather than strained. I sneak glances at Gabriel, and I think he's doing the same—lifting his eyes when he thinks I'm not looking. By all accounts, this should be making me very uneasy, but somehow it's not. It's nice to not be alone.

After a few more minutes, the waitress returns with my breakfast. She slides the plate across the table to rest in front of me. "Can I get you anything else?"

"This looks great," I say. "Thanks."

I follow Gabriel's lead and add a little salt and pepper, then take a bite. He's right, it's delicious in a *this is terrible for you* kind of way.

"I'm just going to admit to my pedestrian tastes in food," I say. "This is so good."

Gabriel laughs. "It is, isn't it? I always feel like I'm not supposed to enjoy it, but *damn* it's a good breakfast."

"I guess you can't always eat fancy food," I say. "How long have you been at the Ocean Mark?"

"I took over about six years ago," he says.

"And you grew up here?"

"I did," he says. "I've lived other places, but I always wanted to come back."

"So you must have family close by?" I ask.

He nods. "My mom lives in town, although to be honest, it's easier if I don't see her too often. She's not bad, just typical judgmental nosy mother stuff. My sister and her husband live here with their little family. I like being able to see my nephews."

Oh man. He has nephews. How cute is that?

"That's sweet," I say. "How old are they?"

"Isaac is seven," he says. "Hunter and Emma adopted him. Their younger son, Sebastian, is a little over a year." He takes another bite of his breakfast. "What about you? Where are you from?"

"Oh, just a little town in Missouri."

"What brought you out here?" he asks.

It's such an innocent question, but it makes me seize up. I consciously unclench my fingers from the handle of my fork and try to make the deep breath I take look casual. "Just needed a change."

His eyes linger on my face, as if he can sense there's

something I'm not telling him. To his credit, he changes the subject, rather than pressuring me for more information. "And how do you like living at the beach so far?"

"It's a nice town," I say. "Moving has been a little overwhelming. It's hard not knowing anyone."

"Well, you know Clover now, which means pretty soon you'll know everyone," he says. "And you know me."

There's that smile again, and the butterflies start doing their thing. I take another bite of my breakfast to cover the sudden flare of shyness.

I'm not sure how to reconcile this gentle, friendly man with the chef who barks orders and scowls at me. There are hints of the chef here—the intensity in his eyes and the way he gets that groove between his eyebrows. But he's much less severe than I first thought.

In fact, far from being uncomfortable, this breakfast has been one of the most pleasant things I've done since I moved.

We chat as we eat, and all too soon, we're both finished. The waitress clears our plates, but we linger over our coffee. Despite this being unexpected, I've had such a nice time. It's been so long since I just sat and talked with someone—especially a man.

The waitress brings our checks and Gabriel takes them both. "Breakfast is on me."

"Thanks," I say. "That's really sweet."

"I'm just bribing you so you won't tell the rest of the staff how much I like eating here."

I laugh. "Your secret is safe with me."

After the waitress brings his change, he leaves a tip on the table and we both get up. He holds the door open for me and we pause on the sidewalk.

"Thanks again," I say. "This was nice."

"Yeah, it was," he says. "I'll see you later, Sadie."

"Bye." I watch him go, feeling a bit awed. I'm not quite sure what happened just now, but it seems my first impression of Gabriel was a little off.

5

GABE

I look at Emma's text again, trying to think of a way out of this. Bowling? Is she serious?

Emma: Hunter's parents are babysitting tonight. We're all going bowling. You're coming.

Me: Maybe another time.

Emma: No isn't an option.

Me: It's my day off and I hate bowling.

Emma: Who cares? Come hang out. Have a beer.

Me: I should probably check in at the restaurant.

Emma: It's your day off. Don't make me come over there.

Me: Yes, mother.

Emma: Good. We're meeting late. See you at ten.

How do I keep getting railroaded by these women in my life? I run my hand through my hair. *We're all going* means a bowling alley full of couples. But if I don't go, I'll probably just wind up back at the restaurant working. Maybe getting out of the house is a better idea.

I wonder what Sadie is doing tonight. It's been a few weeks since her first day at the restaurant. I have to give it to

Clover, Sadie does a great job. She learns fast, she's polite and efficient. Everything I could want in a server.

She's also incredibly distracting. Her thick auburn hair. Her sparkling green eyes. Her fascinating curves. I'm drawn to her; she pulls at me like gravity. There's something mysterious about her; it makes me want to know more. And our spontaneous breakfast at the diner the other day was one of the best hours I've spent in a long time.

Although I have to admit, at work I'm pretty short with her. To be fair, I'm that way with everyone when I'm working. It's my job to make sure the kitchen runs smoothly. I've never worked for a chef who wasn't an asshole, and I do try to tone it down so my staff doesn't hate me.

The strange thing is, I've never worried about it before. When I first brought Clover on, I was hard on her. I wasn't a dick, but I had high expectations, and she's thrived as a chef. Through it all, I never thought twice about what she thought of me. We get along well enough, and she's never been afraid to push back if I get unreasonable.

But I'm constantly wondering what Sadie thinks. I catch myself staring, and then overcompensate by either avoiding her or only giving abrupt responses. I'm trying to make sure I treat her like any other server, but I don't think I'm doing a very good job of it.

Case in point, it wouldn't occur to me to wonder what the rest of my staff are doing tonight. And yet, I can't stop thinking about Sadie.

Shortly before ten I change into jeans and a black t-shirt, then head out to meet everyone.

～

THE AIR in the bowling alley seems stale, almost as if there should be a haze of cigarette smoke hovering over the lanes. The lights are dim and about half the lanes are taken. Bowling balls thunder down the smooth wood, slamming into the pins with sharp cracks, followed by cheers from the bowlers.

I spot Emma and Hunter at a lane on the far side. Hunter looks intimidating, with his huge tattooed arms and straight posture. But he's one of the most easy-going people I know. I wasn't sure if things would work out between him and my sister, but he makes her happy and takes good care of her. There's not much more I could ask for.

Hunter's brothers, Cody and Ryan, are here too. Cody has a protective arm around Clover. He leans in and kisses the top of her head. I've long since given up wondering how two people as different and Cody and Clover ever got together—the doctor and the free spirit. Somehow, they work.

Ryan sits in one of the chairs by the ball return, his wife Nicole perched on his lap. I've known them forever, but I didn't think either of them would wind up living back here in town. But it's been three years since their wedding and they seem to be happily settled. Hunter and I helped Ryan with the addition on their house last year. They live in a small remodeled church not far from my restaurant, and they needed more space when their daughter was born.

As expected, I'm the odd guy out. I consider turning around and going back home, but Emma sees me and waves from the other end of the bowling alley.

I walk over and nod to Hunter, then greet my sister with a hug.

"I'm so glad you came," Emma says.

"Yeah, me too." That's a big fat lie. I realize I'm not fooling her, but I wave to the others and say hello.

"So we were thinking we'd pair off," Emma says. She tucks her blond hair behind her ear and shifts on her feet.

Figures. I lower my voice. "And now you see why I didn't want to come. Do I have to be someone's third? Or play alone?"

"No," she says. "You can play with—"

"Sadie!" Clover exclaims. She darts past me and practically crashes into Sadie, wrapping her in a big hug.

I must look confused—or worse, angry—because Emma nudges me with her elbow and leans in to speak in a low voice. "Don't be grumpy. Clover invited her. Which is good, because she's so sweet, and she doesn't know many people yet."

"Sweet?" I ask. "How would you know?"

"I hung out with her the other day," Emma says.

"How did you even meet her?" I ask.

"Clover," Emma says with a smile, then walks past me to greet Sadie.

Sadie's dressed in a light green top and a pair of curve-hugging jeans. Her red hair is loose around her shoulders. She looks as surprised to see me as I am her.

Emma and Clover introduce Sadie to the others and we all get our bowling shoes from the counter.

"I guess you're with me tonight," I say to Sadie as we put on our shoes.

She meets my eyes and grins. "Looks that way. Do you like bowling?"

I shrug. "I can take it or leave it."

She stands and brushes her hands together. "Well, you better up your game tonight if we're going to be a team. I plan on winning."

The heat in her voice gets my blood pumping. "Does sweet Sadie have a competitive streak?"

"Who said I was sweet?" She smiles again and walks over to where Clover and Cody are choosing bowling balls.

I put on my other shoe and follow her.

Cody seems to be keeping Clover from picking up any of the balls. She has her hands on her hips and rolls her eyes.

"It's just a bowling ball," Clover says.

"But we need to find you a light one," Cody says.

Clover shakes her head and touches her slightly protruding belly. "All right, sexy doctor man."

Sadie picks one up. "What about this one?" She hands it to Cody.

"Nope, too big," Cody says. "Do they have kid sizes?"

Sadie bends over to reach a ball on the lower rack. Shit. Her ass looks fantastic in those jeans. I look away quickly, hoping no one noticed me watching her. She tests out another one, but Cody still deems it too heavy. And there she goes bending over again. I tear my eyes away and go find a ball on an adjacent rack.

Hunter brings over a couple pitchers of beer and a big platter of homemade potato chips while the rest of us get situated in our lane. Nicole sits down to put our names in the scoreboard.

"Okay, first up, Hunter and Emma," she says, but she doesn't type in the name *Hunter*.

"Rambo?" Hunter asks. "He was Army, Nicole. I'm a Marine."

She waves her hand at him. "Just go with it, Stallone."

"Fine, if I'm Rambo, Emma is *Lieutenant Hot Ass*," Hunter says and lightly smacks Emma on the butt.

"Watch it, Rambo," my sister says and gives him a playful

punch to the chest. He wraps his thick arms around her and kisses her while she giggles.

I pinch the bridge of my nose. "For fuck's sake, Hunter."

"Okay, Clover and Cody," Nicole says.

"Call him *Sexy Doctor Man*," Clover says.

Nicole grins and types it in. Then she adds, *Crazy*.

"Crazy? Is that me?" Clover asks. "I'm not crazy."

Everyone swings their gazes to her, eyebrows raised.

"Okay, fine, maybe being pregnant has made me a little bit crazy," she says.

Hunter slings his arm around Emma's shoulders and grins at Clover. "Nope, that's you pretty much all the time, weirdo."

Cody draws her into him and scowls at everyone. "Crazy hot, you mean."

Nicole laughs and types in *Tripod* on the next line.

"Tripod?" Cody asks. "Oh, because Ryan's a photographer."

Nicole smiles, her cheeks flushing. "Yeah, that too."

Ryan stands up straighter, flashing his wife a crooked smile. "And you can be Chesty LaRue."

She laughs and looks down at her chest. "Post-baby boobs for the win."

"Preach, sister," Emma says. They fist bump.

I roll my eyes. These people are killing me.

Nicole types in *Grumpy Smurf* and the other guys snicker. Sadie tries to hide her laugh behind her hand.

"Wait, is that me?" I ask, crossing my arms. "I'm not grumpy. Or blue."

"Well, you're one of those things," Nicole says between giggles. She types in *Red* for Sadie.

Hunter moves closer to me and puts a hand on my

shoulder. "Red, huh? Does that make you the Big Bad Wolf?"

I flinch away from him. "What? No."

Hunter just laughs and pats me on the back.

The game starts and I stand off to the side, feeling kind of awkward. Our turn comes up, and I nod to Sadie to go first. It's impossible not to stare at her ass while she bowls. She gets a spare, and I give her a high five when she comes back.

"Nice work," I say.

"Thanks," she says with a smile.

We both have a drink—the beer isn't bad, considering it's a bowling alley—and snack in between turns. I loosen up as we play. Sadie does indeed have a competitive streak, and she's a pretty good bowler. I do my best to keep up with her. Between the two of us, we keep our team tied for first place with Ryan and Nicole.

I hold my hand up for another high five as Sadie walks back after a strike that puts us in the lead.

"You weren't kidding," I say. "You do plan on winning."

She laughs, a soft tinkling sound. A little bit of the sadness she seems to carry disappears behind the sparkle in her eyes when she smiles. It makes me feel like I'd do anything to make her smile again.

"What can I say? I take my bowling seriously."

"I'm just glad I haven't screwed up," I say. "I don't do this very often."

"You're doing great," she says, touching my arm.

It's just a quick little nudge, but the brief physical contact makes my body ache for more. I nudge her back and wink. She rewards me with another smile. Before I can do anything else, she walks over to the table to get a handful of chips.

I take a deep breath. What am I doing? Hunter's words echo in my mind—*does that make you the Big Bad Wolf*? I've spent the last hour getting increasingly flirtatious with her. I need to remember who she is. Sadie works for me. That means I shouldn't cross the line with her.

Doesn't it?

We finish up the game, Team Grumpy Smurf and Red inching out Ryan and Nicole by five points. I'm tempted to scoop up Sadie in a hug, but I hold back, offering her the millionth high five of the night instead. But she grins at me, her green eyes shining.

Clover decides she's tired, so Cody whisks her out. I'm surprised he doesn't pick her up and carry her, as protective as he's being. The others have to go pick up their kids from Ryan and Hunter's parents. We say goodbye and Sadie and I wander back to our lane. I notice she isn't grabbing her coat, so I don't go for mine.

"Tonight was fun," Sadie says. "How about another game?"

She's right, tonight *was* fun. I haven't laughed this much in a long time. "I have a feeling you'll hand me my ass, but yeah, why not?"

We punch in our names—our real ones this time—to start a new game. I'm as competitive as the next guy, but I'm okay with Sadie beating me. I'm enjoying her company so much, this is a good an excuse as any to keep hanging out with her.

She gets ahead of me in the second frame, and I never recover. But I do enjoy watching her bowl. That woman can gloat all she wants when she's wearing those jeans.

I find reasons to touch her between almost every turn. I nudge her arm or let my hand brush her thigh. Every contact sends a little spark through me, like completing a circuit. I should probably stop, but as the night goes on, it gets harder to remember why. I start to wonder if I can kiss her when I walk her to her car. Maybe invite her out for a drink.

Maybe invite her back to my place.

We finish our game—I don't even want to admit to my abysmal score—and sit to take off our bowling shoes.

"So he can cook, but bowling... maybe not so much," Sadie says with a grin.

"You have me there. I bow to your bowling superiority." I slip my regular shoes back on. "Oh, hey, I needed to mention. I have to switch a couple of your days next week. Sam asked for different days off. I hope that's not a problem."

"Oh... no, that's not a problem at all."

"Great," I say. Now that I'm thinking about the restaurant... "And remind me to show you how I fold the cloth napkins. I have a trick that makes it easier."

"Sure." Her smile is gone and she grabs her bowling shoes. She takes them to the counter without looking back at me. I follow and return mine.

She waits a few feet away while the clerk takes my shoes, fiddling with the zipper on her purse. I thank the guy and she starts walking toward the front. I take a few quick steps to catch up and hold the door open for her.

My heart beats a little faster with anticipation, the words going through my mind, like I need to rehearse them. *Sadie, would you like to go get a drink with me?* Actually, I do need to rehearse them. I'm so out of practice. I can't remember the last time I asked a woman out.

At least, not when I wanted her to say *yes* so badly.

I open my mouth to ask, but she talks first.

"I guess I'll see you at work," she says.

It isn't so much her words, but the way she delivers them that sucks the wind from my sails. She's not looking at me, her eyes on her car, keys already in her hand. Like she's anxious to go.

"Yeah," I say. "Um, thanks for hanging out."

She glances at me with a tight-lipped smile. "Sure. You too. See you at the restaurant, boss."

I shove my hands in my pockets and step back, suddenly feeling like I'm crowding her personal space. I'm not sure what just happened. A few minutes ago, we were all smiles and sparking chemistry. Now she's walking away, her stride quick.

I guess I had the wrong idea.

She gets into her car, and I'm deflated by disappointment. What the hell happened? I didn't think I was coming on too strong. It's not like she could read my mind and see the dirty fantasies I kept having about her.

Her car pulls out of the parking lot, so I head to mine. Figures. Just when I was starting to think there was a little something happening between us, reality comes crashing back. A bowling partner when we're among friends? Fine. But more than that? Nope.

Not for you, Gabriel. You're headed home. Alone.

6

GABE

*A*s much as I would love to put what happened last night out of my mind, I come to work in a terrible mood. When Sadie arrives, it only gets worse. She glances at me when she puts her coat and purse in the back, but quickly looks away. She joins the other servers in getting things ready for tonight, all business, with hardly a look in my direction.

Well, fuck it, then. I don't know what I did to make her turn so cold on me, but if that's how she wants things to be, I'm happy to oblige.

I focus on prepping for tonight's service, and staunchly ignore Sadie.

"What's your problem?" Clover asks out of the blue.

"No problem," I say. "Just working."

"Did you and Sadie stay out last night?" she asks.

"Not for long." Damn it, Clover, I don't want to talk about Sadie.

"Well, how was it?" she asks, her tone conspiratorial.

I shrug. "Fine, I guess."

"Fine, you guess?" she asks. "Gabe, come on. What happened?"

"Absolutely nothing," I say, and walk away from her.

The host seats our first guests and the pace in the kitchen ramps up. We get going on appetizers and I lose myself in the familiar routine of cooking. Sadie comes in and out, and I tell myself a hundred times that everything is normal. Nothing remarkable happened last night. Bowling was fun, but she must have gotten a whiff of my interest in her and promptly backed off. Despite how well we get along, I was clearly seeing what I wanted to see when I thought she might want to extend the evening. I got my hopes up. My mistake.

Dinner orders come in, plates go out. I snap at Clover a few times and she glares at me hard enough that I apologize. We have a full house, but even the busy pace isn't enough to keep my mind off Sadie. I do my best to stay focused and not be too much of an asshole to my staff.

I look over and see Clover talking to Sadie, both of them using hushed voices. Clover looks concerned, with her brow furrowed and hands on her hips.

"What table?" Clover asks.

The anger in Clover's tone makes me pause. What's going on? I inch closer.

"Table seven," Sadie says. "He touches me every time I walk by, but not a lot. Just enough that I can feel it, but not enough that anyone else notices."

"Is he alone?" Clover asks.

"No, his wife is with him."

"Ugh," Clover says. "Horrible. Okay, we'll get Sam to finish up with him. You don't have to talk to him again."

"Are you sure?" Sadie asks. "I don't want to get in trouble."

"Positive," Clover says. "You're fine. Just ignore him and take care of your other tables."

"Thank you," Sadie says.

Clover walks to the other side of the kitchen to talk to Sam. I hesitate as Sadie goes back out to the dining room. I'm seething with fury at the thought of some asshole touching her. I look down and realize I'm clutching a knife, my knuckles white from the strain. With a deep breath, I place the knife gently on the counter.

I move just outside the doorway to the dining room, to a spot where I can watch most of the customers without being intrusive. Usually I pause here to see how a service is going —get a feel for the crowd, so to speak. This time, I watch Sadie as she goes to one of her tables.

There's a couple at table seven. The woman has a black dress and a large diamond necklace at her throat. Her hair is up and her deep red lipstick looks freshly applied. She's busy looking at something on her phone, swiping across the screen with long, manicured fingernails. The man is dressed in a dark suit and blue tie. He rubs his chin, his eyes on Sadie.

I ball my hands into fists and grind my teeth together. I don't care that she's just my employee. I hate that he's even *looking* at her.

Sadie turns to come back to the kitchen, but someone at table eight holds up a hand, flagging her down. She hesitates, her eyes darting to the asshole at seven. She quickly stills her expression and walks by him on her way to see what the customer at eight needs.

My eyes narrow. Sadie stands as far from the guy as she can. He shifts in his chair, straightening his jacket, and reaches out. He can just reach her, and he brushes his hand up the back of Sadie's leg.

Oh fuck no.

Sadie flinches away. I walk out among the tables, my eyes locked on him. Sadie sees me coming and her eyes widen. Her lips part, like she's about to say something, but I put myself between her and the asshole, using my body as a shield to protect her.

The guy raises his eyebrows and opens his mouth, but I don't give a fuck what he has to say.

"Get out of my restaurant," I say, my voice low and quiet. "Now."

Sadie gasps behind me and the guy's mouth curls in a sneer.

"Excuse me?" he asks. His wife looks up from her phone.

"You put your hands on a woman without her permission," I say, straining to keep myself under control. I'm about to punch this guy in the teeth. "I won't stand for that."

"What are you talking about?" he asks. "This guy is crazy."

His wife puts her phone on the table. "What's the meaning of this? What's going on?"

My eyes flick briefly to her. "This man has been harassing one of my servers. He's being asked to leave."

We're starting to cause a scene, which I would normally do almost anything to avoid. But this guy has me so angry I literally have a red haze over my vision.

"That's ridiculous," the woman says. "What are you talking about?"

"I just watched him run his hand up her leg."

"It's okay," Sadie says behind me. "You don't have to—"

I put up my hand to stop her, but I don't take my eyes off the guy. He slowly gets up from his chair.

"Do we have a problem?" he asks.

"There are two ways this ends," I say, still keeping my

voice low. "Either you walk out of here, or I throw your ass out. But you need to get the fuck out of my restaurant. Now."

I don't say another word, and I won't. I stare him down, waiting for him to decide. Finally, he straightens the lapels of his jacket and moves away from the table.

"Let's go, Dana," he says. His wife's eyes are wide and her mouth opens, but she stands and gathers her things.

I don't move until they're both heading for the front door. When they're gone, I take a deep breath. "Please, pardon the interruption," I say, raising my voice to be heard by the tables around me.

Sadie's eyes glisten and she gapes at me. I'm still tense with anger, coiled up like a spring. I touch her gently on the arm and nudge her back toward the kitchen.

"Come on."

She lets me lead her into the back. Everyone is still, like they're frozen, their eyes on me.

"Sam, can you handle Sadie's tables?" I say as we walk toward my office.

"Yes, chef, of course," Sam says.

"Clover, you have the kitchen until I get back."

Clover smiles and gives me a little salute. "Yes, chef."

I still have my hand on Sadie's arm, a light touch on her elbow. I guide her through the kitchen and into my office, then shut the door behind us.

She takes a few steps, keeping her back to me. She hugs her arms around herself and takes deep shuddering breaths.

I look down at the floor, giving us both a minute to calm down. My back is rigid with anger and I have to force myself to relax my fists. I take another long breath.

After several moments of silence, Sadie turns around. "I am so sorry."

"What?" I honestly have no idea what she's talking

about. "What are you sorry for? You didn't do anything wrong."

"I wasn't going to cause a scene," she says, her voice shaky. "I just... he wouldn't stop touching me whenever I walked by. I didn't mean—"

"Stop," I say, my voice as gentle as I can manage. "There is no excuse for what he did to you. No one has the right to harass you like that. I don't care who they are."

She stares at me and swallows hard. Something about the look in her eyes melts me inside. She looks terrified. I don't give two shits about what happened at the bowling alley last night. I want to put my arms around her and hold her against me. I want to tell her I'll protect her, that she doesn't have to be afraid.

"You're not upset with me?" she asks.

"No. Sadie, how could I possibly be upset with you?" I probably shouldn't, but I step closer and take her hand. I lift it and place my other hand on top of hers. "Are you okay?"

"I don't know," she breathes.

I squeeze her hand. "Why don't you go home. The other servers can cover for you."

"Are you sure?" she asks.

"Yes." I should let go of her hand, but she's not pulling away. I want to touch her every time she's near, and now that I am, I don't want to stop. "I'll walk you to your car so you don't have to go outside alone."

"You don't have to do that," she says.

"Yes, I do."

Reluctantly, I drop her hand and move out of her way so she can get her things. I hesitate in my office, making sure I have control over myself. Adrenaline buzzes in my veins. I'm high on more than rage, and I don't want to do something stupid like try to kiss her. Especially after what just happened. The last thing she needs is her boss coming onto her. She already made it clear she's not interested.

She gets her things and I walk her out to her car. I'm so reluctant to let her leave, but what else am I going to do? I have to get back to the kitchen, and she needs to get out of here.

She pauses with her car door open. "Thank you."

"Yeah, of course." She gets in and I close the door behind her.

I watch her leave, still feeling unsettled. Maybe it's all the adrenaline coursing through my system. I head back into the kitchen and try to stay focused on finishing the service. Clover grins at me a few times, but her apparent pride in what I did isn't helping me calm down. All I can think about is Sadie. That haunted look in her eyes. I wish I could have done more to comfort her. I hated sending her off like that.

The rest of the night drags, but eventually the last plates go out. I duck into my office while the servers finish with the guests. I wonder how Sadie is doing. Did she get home okay? Is she still upset about what happened?

I hope she doesn't think she's in trouble. I tried to reassure her, but she seemed so convinced I would be upset with her. Which is ridiculous. But I remember what Clover said on her first day. Sadie got fired from her last job for standing up for herself when a customer harassed her. The fact that it happened to her, again, and in *my* restaurant, makes my blood run hot.

I dig into the file cabinet and find her paperwork. There's a phone number. Maybe I'll just text her to make sure she's okay. There's nothing invasive about that, is there?

Besides, I'm going to go crazy until I know.

I put in her number and send a text.

Me: Hey Sadie, it's Gabriel. Just checking in. Did you make it home OK?

Sadie: Yeah, I did. I'm fine.

I don't believe she's *fine* for one second.

Me: Good. Do you need anything?

Sadie: Thanks, but I don't think so. Did the rest of the service go okay?

Me: It went fine, but seemed to take forever. Long night.

Sadie: I'm really sorry about everything.

Me: Don't. Please. None of that was your fault.

I take another breath. There's more I want to say, but I'm not sure if I should.

Me: It was a long night because I've been worried about you.

Sadie: I'm fine, I promise. I was upset when it happened, but I feel better.

There's a pause and before I can type a reply, she sends another text.

Sadie: I feel better because of you.

I stare at those words on the screen for a long moment. Something about them calms the fire in my veins, slows the beating of my heart. *Because of you.*

Me: That's really good to hear. I wish I could have done more.

Sadie: No, you did everything. I don't know how to thank you.

Me: No thanks necessary. I did what any man would do.

Sadie: No, that's not true. Trust me. You're not just any man.

Thoughts spill through my mind. What else should I say to her? That I wish I was with her right now? That I'd hold her and keep her safe if she'd let me? I'm getting way too close to inappropriate here. But the urge to be with her is so strong.

I glance at her paperwork again. There's an address. Before I can talk myself out if it, I punch it in my phone, grab my coat, and head out the door.

7

SADIE

*T*he house is too quiet, but I'm not ready to get up from my corner of the couch. I'm wrapped in a blanket with my phone still sitting in my hand, wishing Gabriel would text me again.

I'm not sure what I hope he'll say. What else do I want to hear? That he'd like to come over to make sure I'm all right? Of course that's not what I want. That's a ridiculous idea.

Liar. That's exactly what I want.

But there's no way I'm going to ask.

Last night at the bowling alley, I thought something was starting to happen between us. It was both thrilling and scary—but not the kind of scary that makes me want to run. There was all this tension sparking between us—a thousand feelings and desires I didn't think I was capable of feeling anymore.

It didn't escape my notice how often he touched me while we were bowling. And not once did it make me uncomfortable. I don't know what to do with that. Everyone makes me uncomfortable—especially men. But not Gabriel.

When we were taking our shoes off, I thought he might

ask me... something. For my number? To go out for a drink? Maybe a date another night? But instead, he brought up the schedule. And freaking napkins.

Work. Because he's the boss.

There's a clear line between the two of us, and I was embarrassed I'd even considered he might want to cross it. I left abruptly, because I didn't want him to see how flushed my face was. He was just being friendly since we were in a casual situation, but he couldn't be interested in me. I work for him.

Now, I'm not sure what to think. I can't get over what he did tonight. No one has ever stood up for me like that. So many times I've wondered if something is wrong with *me*. Do I attract these kinds of men? Am I asking for it? Should I dress differently? Do I give men the wrong impression with the way I look at them, or the way I speak?

If my therapist knew I was thinking that way again, she'd gently correct me. Remind me to stop blaming myself. But she was the only person in my life who ever suggested that the things that happened to me weren't my fault. It's hard to believe the professional, sitting in a wingback chair with a pen in her hand and a pair of glasses perched on her nose, when your own family is saying something entirely different. That it *was* your fault. That you must have brought it on yourself somehow.

My fucking family. I don't want to think about them. I've limited my contact with them as much as possible without triggering a manhunt to find me. I created an email account that I hope they can't trace to my physical location, and have sent a few messages to let them know I'm alive and doing fine. But other than that, I don't ever want to see them again.

Gabriel, on the other hand...

The asshole at table seven tonight almost made me lose

it. I had a sick feeling in the pit of my stomach from the moment I took his first drink order. He looked me up and down like I was on the menu, even though his wife was sitting right there. She hardly paid attention—her eyes were glued to her phone.

The first time his fingers brushed the back of my leg, I thought I imagined it. But the look on his face told me otherwise. I was nauseated and terrified—afraid to even go back out into the dining room.

I hoped once Clover asked Sam to handle the table, I wouldn't have to worry anymore. But that fucking prick reached out and touched me *again*. I was half a second away from spinning around and clocking him in the face—and certainly losing yet another job—when Gabriel appeared.

His face was a storm cloud of anger, nearly stopping my heart. For a second, I was afraid he was coming out to yell at me—in front of a dining room full of guests, no less. He couldn't possibly be gunning for a paying customer with such murderous eyes. But he stepped in between me and the customer like he was a shield, cutting me off from the guy's advances.

It felt like being in a dream, watching the man and his wife angrily get up and leave. A wall of strong, immovable man stood between me and my harasser. I was so overwhelmed, I couldn't have spoken a word in that moment if my life had depended on it.

But Gabriel didn't stop there. He ushered me into the back, leading me into the privacy of his office. And then he did something that was almost as amazing as kicking out that customer.

He gave me space.

He didn't rush to ask if I was okay—which clearly I was not. He didn't pelt me with questions about what the hell happened, or demand I explain myself. He just stood behind me, silent and protective, waiting until I could collect myself.

My phone vibrates with another text and I almost drop it. I swallow hard and check, hoping against hope it's another message from Gabriel. It is.

Gabriel: I'm outside. I won't bother you if you want to be alone, but I thought maybe you could use some company.

I pause for a moment, staring at the screen. He's here? I listen and can just hear the hum of an engine. He must be parked on the street. I would have heard if he pulled into my driveway.

I'm overcome with gratitude that he's here, but I wonder... should I invite him to come in? That would mean being alone with a man. A man I don't know very well.

Although sometimes the people you know best do the most damage.

Me: Sure, that would be nice.

I get up and open the door, watching as he gets out of his car and comes down the driveway. I'm not prepared for a guest, and I have a fleeting worry as to what my hair must look like. But it all disappears when I see the soft expression in his eyes as my porch light illuminates his face. My heart flutters and a little swirl of nervousness fills my tummy. Such a different feeling from the fear I often feel when standing face to face with a man. There's no sense of wanting to run, no adrenaline coursing through my veins.

He stops a few feet in front of me. "I'm sorry to show up unannounced like this. Maybe I should have called first, but I was afraid you'd say no."

I probably would have. I would have said I was fine, not

wanting to be a bother. But I'm so glad he's here. "You don't need to apologize. Come in."

I step back so he can come inside and close the door behind him, making sure to lock the deadbolt and the chain lock above it.

"Can I get you anything?" I gesture to the couch and he sits.

"No," he says. "I'm fine. I just wanted to make sure you're okay."

No. I'm emotionally exhausted and I have been for so long. "Yeah, I'm fine." I sit down next to him, leaving a bit of space between us.

"Sadie, I am so sorry about tonight," he says. "I've only had a customer behave that way once before. That isn't the type of establishment I run."

I gape at him, my lips parted. *He's* apologizing to *me*? "It's certainly not your fault."

"I know," he says. "But I feel responsible."

Of course. He's here as my boss. It happened in his place of business and he probably wants to make sure I won't try to sue him or something.

"It's okay," I say. "I don't blame you or the restaurant. You don't have to worry about anything."

"The only thing I'm worried about is you," he says.

He reaches out and touches my hand. It's such a simple gesture—friendly, not the least bit aggressive. And if it was any other man in the world, it would send me into a tailspin of panic.

But just like every other time he's touched me, I'm not startled or unnerved by the feel of his hand on mine. I can't remember the last time I could be touched without bracing myself for it, as if every instance of human contact is like a car accident to my psyche. Even a simple handshake requires a second or two of mental preparation. I've come to accept this as simply the way things are. I'm irreparably broken, and this is one of the manifestations of my brokenness.

Yet, when Gabe rests his hand on mine, I feel comfort. Assurance. Trust.

And something else, opening within me like the petals of a flower in the spring sunshine.

Hope.

Tears sting my eyes and I bite the inside of my lip to keep from crying. How can I feel something so intensely for a man I barely know? A man who arguably isn't always that nice to me. Who can't possibly be feeling the same things I am.

Although he's never treated me *badly*—not really. He can be brusque when we're working. But I've worked in restaurants before, and he's one of the better-tempered chefs I've known. And what he did for me tonight...

I turn my hand so my palm faces his. He gently squeezes it and rubs his thumb along the vulnerable skin on the inside of my wrist. I take a trembling breath and try to swallow back the tears, but I'm overcome. The cords I keep wound so tight around my emotions loosen, and a shuddering sob escapes my throat.

Without a word, Gabriel draws me into his arms. They wrap around me, solid, strong, protective. I relax against him and let the tears come.

He holds me while I cry, while I dampen his shirt with my tears. His hands rub gentle circles on my back and he rests his cheek against my hair. I couldn't stop the flood of emotion if I wanted to, but letting it out feels good. I can't remember the last time someone held me like this. I've missed this feeling so much.

Gabriel settles back against the cushions and I tuck my feet up. I rest my head against his chest, his arms still wrapped around me. The tears finally stop, but he doesn't let go. My breathing slows and the tension in my body melts away. We don't say a word. He simply holds me, as if he somehow knows how badly I needed this.

I'm sure he thinks my distress is all because of what happened at work. A part of me wants to tell him the truth —tell him everything I've been through. But what if he doesn't believe me? What if my story sounds too impossible to be real? It would be hard to blame him. My own family thought I was lying. How could I expect *him* to see the truth?

And I don't think I can bear that kind of rejection again.

So I stay silent and lose myself in the simple comfort of a man's strong arms around me.

I WAKE WITH A START, panic seizing my chest, making it hard to breathe. My eyes dart around the room as I try to center myself. I'm in my room. My bed. Alone. It's dark and I glance at the clock. It's just after four.

How did I get here?

The last thing I remember is drifting off to sleep on the couch with Gabriel's arms around me. Oh god, I can't believe I fell asleep on him. I glance beneath the sheets. I'm still dressed, and I have a vague memory of being carried to bed. Did Gabriel bring me here? How did I sleep through that?

Panic grips me again. The locks. If Gabriel put me to bed, no one was up to lock the door when he left.

I fly out of bed, but stop in front of my closed bedroom door. My heart beats fast and adrenaline courses through my body. *Be calm, Sadie. Be calm.* Even if the door isn't locked, no one will be out there. Adam isn't suddenly going to appear out of nowhere just because the door is unlocked for one night.

With a deep breath, I open the door.

Someone *is* out there, but it's not Adam Cooper. It's Gabriel.

He's lying on the couch with his head on a throw pillow, his eyes closed. I pause, not wanting to wake him, but his eyes drift open.

"Hey," he says, his voice thick with sleep. He sits up.

"I'm sorry, I didn't mean to wake you," I say.

He rubs his eyes. "Don't worry about it. What time is it?"

"Around four."

"Do you want me to go?"

"No, I…" I pause, staring at him. Why did he stay?

As if he can read my thoughts, he answers my unasked question. "I just wanted you to feel safe."

I let out a shuddering breath and a few tears break free from the corners of my eyes. The last thing I want to do is cry again, but I'm overcome. *I just wanted you to feel safe.*

Gabriel stands and an instant later, I'm in his arms again.

"I'm sorry," I say into his chest. "I got up to be sure the door was locked."

He squeezes me tighter. "It's fine. Let's get you back to bed."

I wipe the tears from my cheeks and let him lead me into my room. My body aches with exhaustion, the mental and emotional strain weighing heavily on me. I get in bed and Gabriel pulls up the covers.

"I'll be right out there," he says. "You don't have to worry about anything tonight."

He turns to go, but I reach out and grab his hand. My

heart still beats uncomfortably hard, pounding against my ribs. I desperately don't want to be alone. "Could you... could you stay here?"

"Sure, if you want me to," he says, his voice quiet in the darkness.

He glances around like he's looking for a blanket and I realize he's about to lie down on the floor. I can't ask him to sleep on the floor, and I certainly don't want him to. At this point, I don't care if this isn't appropriate. I lift the covers and scoot over, making room.

"Are you sure?" he asks.

I nod and he gets in bed with me. For a second it seems like he'll settle in with space between us. But he looks at me with a furrowed brow and reaches out to pull me in close. My body molds against his and my tired eyes close. In minutes, my heart rate slows and I relax, feeling nothing but the safety and security of Gabriel's arms.

8

SADIE

I wake to the weight of Gabriel's arm slung over me. My back is to his front, my body tucked against him. I close my eyes and try not to think about what we're going to say to each other later. For now, I just want to live in this moment.

I can't remember the last time I slept so well. I peek at the clock; it's eight thirty. It was only about four hours ago that he came to bed with me, but I feel more rested than I have in months. The soft sound of his breathing and the warmth of his body did more to help me sleep than anything else I've ever tried.

And I've tried just about everything.

He stirs, drawing in a deep breath, and his body jerks a little. I think he just realized where he is—and who he's with. I keep still, pretending to be asleep, hoping he might not move. Hoping he wants to stay this way a little longer too.

At first, it seems like he's going to try to extricate himself. His arm shifts and he starts to roll away. But then he moves back, drawing his arm around me again. He inhales deeply, smelling my hair. I squeeze my eyes shut, willing my body to stay relaxed.

God, this feels so good. I didn't think I was capable of enjoying this feeling anymore. I thought it had been taken from me. The idea that I can reclaim this—that I can enjoy the embrace of a man—is so stunning, so unexpected, I'm not sure what to do with myself. I'm halfway between laughing and crying, all the while trying to hold everything in so I don't break the spell.

But I can't lie still forever. I enjoy the feel of him for long moments, but eventually I have to move. I act like I'm just waking up, hoping that helps dispel any awkwardness he might feel.

He backs off immediately, lifting his arm and moving away.

I look at him over my shoulder and smile. "Good morning."

"Morning," he says. "Did you get some rest?"

"I slept really well, actually." I turn over so I'm facing him. "Thank you."

He gives me that smile again—his secret smile. "It's no problem. Are you feeling better?"

"Yes, a lot better," I say. "I'm sorry I was such a mess last night."

"You really need to stop apologizing for things," he says. "You had a rough night. You should have been a little messy."

Oh Gabriel, you have no idea how messy I really am. "Yeah, I guess so. Thank you again for coming over."

"I just wanted to make you feel better," he says.

"You did," I say. "So much better."

He smiles again and for a second, I think he's going to

lean in and kiss me. There's not much distance between us. He could easily move closer and bring his lips to mine.

But he doesn't. He rolls away and sits up. "I should probably get home. I have to be at work early."

I try to swallow back the disappointment that rolls through me. "Right, of course."

"Ordinarily, I'd love to make you breakfast or something," he says. "But the people from *Simple Pleasures* are coming today. I think I'm supposed to meet with them at ten. I'm not looking forward to it, but I need to get it out of the way."

Sam told me last week about the feature *Simple Pleasures* is doing on Gabriel and the restaurant. It sounds like a great opportunity for him, but did it have to be today? Although thinking about it reminds me of something I needed to ask.

"Are they going to be taking pictures?" I ask. "I mean, I'm sure they'll want photos of you, and of the restaurant. But what about the rest of the staff?"

"I'm not sure," he says. "Probably."

"I'd just prefer it if I'm not in any of them," I say. I really don't want to explain why. I watch Gabriel's face, bracing myself for what he'll ask, my mind spinning with possible explanations.

"Sure, I'll let them know," he says.

My lips part in surprise. That's it? He doesn't want to interrogate me about it? "Thank you. I'd appreciate that."

"Are you sure you're ready to come back to work tonight?" he asks.

"Yes," I say, emphatic. "I'm not letting some handsy dickbag keep me from my job."

He laughs. "Good for you." He moves the covers and stands, but pauses, looking back at me. "Hey, there's a new winery I need to go check out tomorrow. Maybe you'd like to join me?"

My breath catches in my throat. Does he mean, like, a date? I'm not sure, but I surprise myself with how quickly I answer. "Sure, that sounds fun."

"Great," he says. "Do you drink wine? They'll do a private tasting for us, and I could use another opinion. I'm thinking of sourcing from them for the restaurant."

"Yes, I drink wine," I say, trying to keep my disappointment to myself. There's the boss again. Not a date. He just needs another taster and he must know I happen to be off work tomorrow.

He smiles again. "I'll confirm the time with them and text you when I know for sure. I can drive, if you don't mind."

"Sure."

"I'm just going to use your bathroom, and then I should get going."

I nod and get up, grabbing a hair tie from my nightstand. I pull my hair up and tie it off in a messy bun. This girl needs some coffee so I can sort through what happened last night—and this morning. I'm so grateful Gabriel came over, and I could sure get used to sleeping so soundly. I do like the idea that maybe we're a little more than boss and employee. That we're friends, at least. So even if the winery isn't a date, it will be nice to spend time with him.

And if I'm wrong, and it is a date...

But I shouldn't get my hopes up. And I'm not sure I'm ready for that anyway.

Gabriel leaves and I decide to veg out and do nothing with my day before I have to work. I figure I've earned some zone out in front of the TV time.

At two-thirty, I head to the restaurant. When I come in

through the back door, nothing seems out of the ordinary. I was half expecting a camera crew to be getting in everyone's way, but there's only staff in the kitchen. Gabriel is nowhere in sight.

I get to work, helping prep for tonight's service. I catch a glimpse of Gabriel sitting with someone at a table on the far side of the dining room. A man with a camera stands nearby. He points it at Gabriel and takes a picture.

The kitchen is a whirlwind of activity, as it always is in the hour before guests begin arriving. Gabriel walks in a short time later, followed by the guy with the camera. A woman walks in behind them and I'm hit with a pang of jealousy so strong it nearly knocks the breath from my lungs.

She's gorgeous. Not normal-person gorgeous. Stunning. She's tall and slender, dressed in a perfectly tailored blouse tucked into a slim pencil skirt. Her hair is so dark it's almost black, and it shines like she just walked off the set of a high-end shampoo commercial. Perfect bone structure. Perfect makeup. Perfect teeth when she smiles. She turns that breathtaking smile on Gabriel and I want to rip her throat out.

I turn away quickly so I don't stand here glaring at her. There's no reason for me to lose my mind with envy. She's just here to interview Gabriel about the restaurant. Who cares if she looks like she belongs on the cover of *Vogue*?

Or, with those boobs, *Maxim*.

And it isn't like anything is going on between me and Gabriel. Yes, he slept in my bed with me last night. My cheeks warm at the memory. But I have no claim on him.

I look up and see Gabriel smiling at her. My stomach turns over. This is going to be a long night.

Gabriel isn't working; Clover is heading the kitchen. But he does spend time cooking so the photographer can take pictures. He takes some of the dining room as well. I make sure to stay out of the way and try to focus on my job. It's a weeknight, and we're not fully booked, so the pace isn't too hectic. My guests are all pleasant, happy with the food and the service.

About halfway through the evening, the woman— apparently her name is Alice Hudson—and the photographer disappear, as does Gabriel. I start to wonder why I felt such a strange surge of jealousy. It's so unlike me. The more time that goes by, the sillier I feel. By the end of my shift, I have my head back on straight.

And I have the winery to look forward to tomorrow.

MY MORNING GOES by with all the speed of a garden snail. By eleven, I haven't heard from Gabriel, but I've been up, showered, and ready for hours.

Finally, my phone *bings* with a text. I smile as I swipe the screen.

Gabriel: I'm really sorry, but I'm going to have to cancel the winery trip today. Another time?

My heart sinks and my shoulders slump. I feel so deflated.

I wish I wasn't so disappointed, but I spent my whole morning looking forward to this. And the wine had very little to do with it. I sigh and put my phone down, wondering why he'd cancel. He didn't give a reason. Is he going to? Minutes pass and he doesn't reply. I guess that's it —he just can't?

About half an hour later, my phone does *bing*, but it's not a text from Gabriel. It's Clover, inviting me to join her for lunch. Grateful for the distraction, I agree and head out to meet her at Old Town Café.

I find Clover already seated at a table near the window. She waves as I walk over and sit down across from her.

"Hey," she says. "Thanks for meeting me."

"Of course," I say. "Thanks for inviting me."

She smiles and I have to admit, being here is already lifting the haze of disappointment.

"So," she says, "tell me honestly. How are you liking your job?"

"I like it a lot," I say, and that's the truth. I don't know that I want to wait tables for the rest of my life, but I do enjoy my job. "The people are great, and the restaurant is amazing. Maybe this sounds weird, but I feel kind of at home there."

"That doesn't sound weird at all," she says. "Of course it does. You were obviously meant to be there."

That's not the first time Clover has mentioned some sort of metaphysical reason for me moving to Jetty Beach and landing a job at the Ocean Mark. I don't believe in that sort of thing, but Clover seems to, so I just smile and go along with it.

"Well, meant to be or not, I'm happy working there," I say. "Yesterday was kind of uncomfortable with the magazine people around. But at least that's over."

"Thankfully they weren't too intrusive," Clover says. "And Alice was nice."

Could have done with less cleavage. "Yeah, she seemed to be. So how are you feeling?"

Clover takes a deep breath. "Pregnancy is the weirdest thing. So far I haven't had any morning sickness, but I'm more tired than usual. Cody is bugging me to cut back on the days I work. But mostly I just want to binge on pink Starburst and strawberry pineapple smoothies."

"Cravings, huh?"

"Like you wouldn't believe," she says. "Oh, and anything sour. I literally sucked a lemon dry the other day."

I laugh. "That sounds awful."

"You'd think," she says. "Cody couldn't even watch me do it, he was so grossed out."

"Sorry, but I think I'm with Cody," I say. "Is he excited?"

She smiles and the warmth in her eyes makes my heart bleed a little. "He's so excited. He made this little calendar on our fridge with all the pregnancy milestones. Some mornings we come downstairs and look at it and say hey, our baby is the size of my pinky finger today! It's adorable. He's going to be the best daddy."

"I bet he is," I say.

"What about you?" she asks. "Do you think you want kids someday?"

"I..." I falter, unsure of how to answer that question. There was a time it would have been an easy *yes*. I always figured I'd have children. But now... "I'm not sure, to be honest. I'm a few steps behind in that department, considering I'm single."

"Yeah, of course," Clover says. "I was just curious. I wasn't sure if I wanted kids until I met Cody."

"But then you were sure?" I ask.

She smiles. "Yes. Very sure."

"You two are so sweet," I say. "You make me think love actually exists."

Clover tilts her head. "Of course love exists. You'll find it. I'm positive. And I'm always right about these things."

"Thanks," I say. "I'm happy being on my own."

Am I really, though? There's a certain safety in being

alone. If I don't let anyone get too close, I can't get hurt. Trust is hard to come by and so easily broken.

"Well, life can surprise you sometimes," she says with a little shrug. "Thanks for meeting me, by the way. I was hoping to catch Gabe today, but I guess he took Alice out to that new winery."

It feels like my heart stops beating entirely. He took *her* to the winery? That's why he canceled on me? A sick feeling swirls in the pit of my stomach, but I do my best to keep it from showing. "Oh, I thought the magazine people were gone."

"No, they stayed last night," she says. "I guess Alice wasn't done with Gabe."

Stayed last night. Oh my god. Stayed where? Did that hussy stay with Gabriel? They left the restaurant around the same time. That must be why he invited her to the winery. If he slept with her last night, he probably wanted to spend more time with her. Taking a beautiful journalist to the winery sure beats bringing your plain, redheaded waitress along.

It's almost impossible to keep my disappointment inside, but I manage to have a pleasant lunch with Clover. When it's over, I head home. The last few days have been such a roller coaster, I'm not sure what to think anymore.

9

GABE

$\mathcal{T}$he winery grounds are beautiful, and the weather is perfect. You couldn't ask for a better day for a tour and tasting. A few puffy white clouds float across the bright blue sky, and the view of the vineyard is spectacular. The main building is nice; it has a classic style with rustic touches—rich wood, leather seating, low light. After we tour the facility and get an overview of their operation, we're led to the tasting room. It's cozy and intimate, with comfortable stools at the dark wood bar.

It would be a perfect afternoon, except for the company.

Granted, Alice Hudson, up-and-coming journalist for *Simple Pleasures*, is a beautiful woman. Any man who can't admit that is lying. Lush dark hair, full breasts, legs that go on for miles. She's dressed in a pair of tan slacks and a white blouse that's open just enough to reveal the valley between her breasts.

Regardless of what she looks like, Alice Hudson is not who I wanted to bring with me to the winery today.

I thought she was finished with the interview yesterday at the restaurant. She asked me about everything from my early love of cooking, to my education, to the progression of my career. I was pleased that she kept the focus entirely on the restaurant itself, and me as a chef. She asked almost no personal questions at all. Nothing about my failed marriage, or my current relationship status.

I met with her for several hours. When she and the photographer, a soft-spoken guy named Ricardo, left, I assumed we were finished.

This morning, I was in my office, catching up on some things with Linda, when Alice called. She said she'd gone over her notes last night and had some follow up questions. Linda could hear our conversation, and she nodded at me, her eyes giving me a clear message: Keep being nice and do what she asks.

I already had a tour set up at the winery, so it seemed like the only way to get this over with would be to use the time to finish the interview with Alice.

Which meant I had to cancel with Sadie.

It was physically difficult to write that text. I started out trying to explain what was going on, but it was turning into the longest text in the history of mankind. So I kept it short, just letting her know I was sorry and I'd see her soon.

The second I hit send, I regretted doing it, and I've regretted it ever since.

Alice and I didn't talk much while on the tour; we were busy listening to the winery manager. We made small talk while we sampled a few of their wines, but Alice didn't get into her questions.

Now we're sitting out on a terrace in the warm sunshine with a cheese spread and a bottle of their chardonnay. The wine is fantastic—I think they have varieties that will pair beautifully with many of our dishes. But this trip is dragging on longer than I anticipated. I keep wanting to check my phone to see if Sadie responded to my text—she hadn't by the time I picked Alice up at her hotel. But I don't want to be rude.

Alice swirls the wine in her glass. "This is lovely. Thank you again for inviting me along."

"You're welcome." I hope she gets to her questions. I'm ready for this to be over, but Linda's voice keeps echoing in my head, reminding me not to be an asshole.

"So, Gabe," she says, "it seems like the life of a chef must be quite busy. Does your work take up a great deal of your time?"

I hesitate for a beat, wondering if she's going to take out her phone or a notepad to take notes, but she just watches me, her wineglass still in her hand. "I suppose it does. I'm called a workaholic a lot."

"Addicted to your work," she says. "Maybe passion and addiction are simply two sides of the same coin."

"Could be," I say.

She licks her lips, slowly, like she wants me to notice. I do, but if she's trying to flirt with me, it's not having the desired effect.

"What do you like to do in your free time?" she asks.

"I like to cook. I know that sounds strange, but I spend a lot of time experimenting at home." Or I used to, before I got the chef's version of writer's block.

"Experimenting," she says, her mouth twitching in a smile. "That's very... enticing."

"It's how I keep the menu fresh," I say, trying to keep us both on topic. I'm pretty sure she wasn't thinking about food when she said the word *experimenting*.

"Of course," she says. "What else?"

"Honestly, Alice, there's not much else to tell," I say. "I go running. Lift weights at the gym. I hang out with friends. I have family who live in town. I like to see my nephews."

"Hmm," she says, a soft purring sound at the back of her throat. "No one at home to cook for?"

I glance away. "No, I live alone."

"I'm sorry. I touched a nerve," she says.

"No, it's fine," I say.

"Gabe, I do this for a living," she says. "I can see when I've hit on something tender. I won't press you about it. We all have our sad stories. I'm not looking to uncover yours."

I meet her eyes again. "Thank you."

"Does it help if I tell you I'm glad to hear there isn't someone in particular who has the pleasure of tasting all your... creations?"

I take a sip of my wine. "It's still not something I'm interested in discussing."

"All right," she says, putting her glass down. "But this passion, or addiction, you have for your work. Does it interfere with your personal life?"

"Sometimes."

"So vague," she says with another twitch of her lips.

"I suppose I like to keep my personal life private," I say.

She leans forward, slowly, and her breasts press against her blouse. "This isn't part of the interview, Gabe."

I take another drink to give myself a second to think. I can tell she's a woman who's accustomed to getting what she wants, particularly from men. She has the confident vibe of someone who rarely hears the word *no*. I'm familiar with the type. My ex-wife was exactly like her.

Maybe I can steer this back toward interview territory. "Yes, my work does interfere with my personal life. But I love what I do, so the trade-off is worth it."

"I understand exactly what you mean." She trails her

finger around the rim of her wineglass. "I have the same problem. You could say I have a similar passion—or perhaps addiction—to my work. It doesn't afford me a lot of time for a personal life."

"I guess we're all striving for balance," I say.

"Well said. I think finding balance means we need to indulge ourselves once in a while." She raises her glass, as if she's referring to the wine, but I see right through the gesture.

"And a winery is the perfect place for it," I say.

Her dark brown eyes hold onto mine, her expression sultry and intense. "My hotel room isn't a bad spot either."

Oh, shit.

"Alice, I—"

"Gabe, I'm going to level with you," she says. "I think we're both a little lonely. I'm in town one more night." She slides her tongue out across her lips again. "I can make it a night you'll never forget."

It's extremely telling that my dick is doing nothing— literally nothing—in my pants. Not a twitch of interest. You'd think if an objectively beautiful woman—because, for fuck's sake, she has everything going for her—offers a night of no-strings sex, any man's cock would stand up and take notice. Mine? Nothing.

And even if I was straining against my pants, my answer would be the same.

"Thank you, Alice, that's... tempting." That's a lie. "But I don't think that would be a good idea."

Her eyebrows lift, a slight movement that momentarily betrays her surprise. In mere seconds, her face smooths out again. "I assure you, it's a very good idea. And in case I'm not making myself clear, I'll be gone tomorrow. I just want a taste of your... talents. Nothing more."

It hits me as I stare at my almost-empty wine glass that I picked her up at her hotel. I have to drive her back to town. Do I give her a hard no right here, and deal with the awkwardness of the drive? Or be noncommittal until we get back to town?

"I think we're about done with our wine, don't you?" I stand, not waiting for her answer.

Her eyebrows draw together, like she's not sure what I mean. But she stands and shoulders her purse. "Yes, I'm finished."

"Great, I'll get you back to your hotel."

We walk to my car and my back is so tense I feel like I might snap. I don't know if my last comment got my point across, or if she thinks I'm going to take her up on her offer. There's no way I'm spending the night with Alice. Attractive or not, I'm not interested, even if it's just for a night of sex. Granted, I've been single for a long time, so a night of sex would be fucking fantastic.

But not with Alice.

Don't even get me started on the fact that all I can think about is Sadie. I have no idea what to do with that.

We pass most of the drive back to town in silence. I'm stiff and uncomfortable, but I keep my eyes on the road, working out what I'm going to say to Alice when we get to her hotel. I suddenly realize why girls in bars often make up fake boyfriends to ward off unwanted advances. It's an easy fall back; I wish I could claim that I'm seeing someone as an excuse. But I already admitted I'm not.

Although, Sadie...

What about Sadie? What can I claim that she is to me? My employee. Perhaps my friend. I spent a night holding her, but what did I do then? Nothing. My entire body ached with the desire to kiss her when we woke up together yesterday morning. I wish I would have.

She was beautiful. Her hair a tangled mess, smelling like jasmine. Little smudges of makeup on her cheeks from crying. Her body warm and soft against mine as we slept. I would have done just about anything for more time with her. But I had to get to work.

I never should have agreed to this with Alice. I should have told her I wasn't available. Then it would be Sadie sitting beside me now. Sadie in my passenger seat, racing down the highway toward town. I bet the wine would have flushed her cheeks. The view would have made her smile.

I pull into the hotel parking lot and I'm jolted from my thoughts by the feeling of something on my leg. Alice's perfectly manicured hand rests on my thigh, just above my knee.

"The offer still stands," she says, her voice low. She squeezes my leg. "Come up. Trust me. You'll be glad you did."

I breathe out a long breath. "Alice, thank you, but I'm afraid I can't."

She gapes at me, her full lips open. If she's anything like my ex—and I think these two might as well be long lost twins—she's accustomed to getting her way. "Gabe, if you have any concerns about tomorrow, let me assure you, there's no need. I just want you to fuck me in every way you can think of tonight. And then we'll go our separate ways."

Okay, that gets a twitch out of my dick. I'm a guy, after all, and I'm only human. But there's just no way. "I understand you completely. But the answer is still no."

With a sharp jerk of her neck, her face turns forward. She gathers up her purse and opens the car door. "Your loss, I suppose."

The door shuts with a loud bang. She didn't quite slam it, but she shut it hard enough to let me know she's angry. I grip the steering wheel and drive away. That was a shit show. I wonder her article is going to say now?

Nothing I can do about it at this point. Even Linda would have drawn the line at me sleeping with Alice to get good PR.

What a fucking day. I check my phone again, but Sadie never did respond. Damn it, I fucked this up royally.

Maybe I shouldn't, but I turn toward Sadie's house.

10

SADIE

*W*hat is it about ice cream that makes it the universal *I've had a shitty day and want to wallow in it* food? I'm not sure, but I'm sitting on my couch with a pint of Ben and Jerry's—Chunky Monkey, thank you very much—and a glass of wine. It's a weird combination, and the fact I'm craving French fries makes it worse. I was tempted to go into town and find a place where I could get both—fries and a milkshake would have been ideal—but the thought of sitting pathetically alone in a restaurant was enough to keep me home.

The spoonful of ice cream chills my mouth with creamy, sugary goodness. But it's not really making me feel better. Comfort food often sounds like a good idea, but it doesn't usually pan out.

After having lunch with Clover, I tried very hard to get my head together and stop thinking about Gabriel. Not an easy task, considering it's my day off, and I was supposed to be with him today. I didn't exactly have fallback plans. I wound up scrubbing my house clean from top to bottom until I was too exhausted to continue.

And now a date with my old loves, Ben and Jerry.

I take another bite. "You two are always here for me when I need you."

From outside, I hear the rumble of an engine. It slows and turns off. Seconds later, a knock at my door.

The sound makes every muscle in my body contract painfully. The next breath feels labored and a cold sweat breaks out on my forehead.

With shaking hands, I put the ice cream and spoon on the coffee table. Who would come over unannounced? I check my phone, but I don't have any texts or messages. There are only a few people who know where I live, and I'm not expecting anyone.

Calm down, Sadie. I take a deep breath. I hate that something as simple as a knock at my door rattles me like this. But my chest feels constricted, like I can't get enough air. I'm on the verge of hyperventilating and my heart knocks against my ribs.

Another deep breath and I focus on the feel of the air expanding my lungs. I look at the door, with the deadbolt, and a chain lock I installed myself. No one is getting through that bad boy unless I open it for them.

My hands aren't shaking as badly when I stand and go over to the door. Whoever it is knocks again—which isn't a surprise, considering it's taking me so long to get myself together to even ask who it is. But the noise jolts me just the same.

"Who is it?" I call through the door.

The reply is muffled. "It's Gabriel."

The sound of his voice does funny things to my insides, so unlike the rush of fear when he first knocked.

But why on Earth is he here?

It takes me another few seconds to decide what to do.

I'm shaken at having someone show up out of the blue, and I honestly don't know if I can face him right now. All I can see is *her*. I hate that I feel so catty about it, but I thought...

It doesn't matter what I thought. I was wrong.

"Is everything okay?" I ask through the door.

"Yeah," he says. "Can I talk to you?"

I slide out the chain lock, unlatch the deadbolt, and unlock the doorknob. I open the door to find Gabriel, dressed in a light blue button down with the sleeves cuffed, and dark jeans. I glance down at myself. Not only am I wearing faded yoga pants and an oversize t-shirt, I have a drip of ice cream just over my left boob.

"Hey," he says.

I hesitate, not quite sure if I'm going to invite him in. He doesn't make a move to come inside, just watches me, clearly awaiting my go-ahead.

The fact that he waits—that he's not barging in without my permission—is what tips the scales in his favor.

"Hi." I step aside and motion for him to come in.

I shut the door behind him and lock all three locks. He takes a quick look around and I can tell he notices my container of ice cream, the spoon still sticking straight out the top.

God, I'm such a mess.

"Listen, Sadie," he says, but pauses, looking at the floor, like he's trying to work out what to say. "I owe you an apology for canceling today."

I shrug and sit back down, grabbing my ice cream. I'm wearing some on my shirt; might as well own it. "It's fine. You were busy."

He sits down next to me. "No, it's not fine. I was really looking forward to it. The way things turned out..." He shakes his head.

The way things turned out? What is that supposed to mean? "Things didn't go well at the winery? Wasn't Alice pleasant enough company?"

His eyes snap to mine. He didn't realize I knew. "No. No, she wasn't, as a matter of fact."

"You didn't seem to have any complaints last night."

"Last night?" he asks, his brow furrowed.

I shrug, trying to act like it's no big deal, and take another bite of ice cream. "It looked like you were getting along very well when you left the restaurant together."

He blinks, his gaze traveling between the ice cream in my hands, to my face, back again. "You thought...? No, we left at the same time, but I didn't leave *with* her. I went home last night. Alone."

The spoon dangles from my fingers, just above the container. "You did?"

"Yes, very much alone."

"Then why... why did you take her to the winery today?"

He sighs. "She called this morning and said she had more questions for me. Linda has been on me to be cooperative. I assumed they were leaving town soon, so I figured the only way to get it done would be to see her at the winery."

I stare down at the ice cream in my hands. So he didn't... They didn't...

"How did you know I was there with her?" he asks.

"I had lunch with Clover."

He nods. "I shouldn't be surprised. Listen, I didn't want to be there with her. And she didn't really want to interview me anyway. She just wanted to get personal."

"I can only imagine," I say.

"I regretted canceling all day," he says, his voice going soft. "I would have much rather been there with you."

My heart is still beating too fast and my hands tremble. He has me so unsteady. I spent half the day thinking he'd ditched me for a hot piece of ass. Now he shows up here, at my house, to tell me he didn't? And that he wishes he hadn't canceled on me?

"Well, maybe another time," I say.

His eyebrows lift. "Could there be another time?"

I dig the spoon into the ice cream, my eyes intent on it, like it's suddenly very interesting. "Is this a work thing? For the restaurant? Or do you mean like... a date?"

He shifts closer. "I mean a date."

I meet his eyes, feeling a little surge of bravery. "Was the winery supposed to be a date?"

"Yes. With you, it was." He swallows. "I guess I didn't do a good job of making that clear. I'm a little out of practice."

His sheepish little grin and sparkling eyes melt me. "Okay, then. I'd like that."

He takes the ice cream out of my hands and sets it on the coffee table. I swallow hard as he leans in close. My tongue darts out across my lips, moving as if it has a mind of its own.

A tingle of fear hits me. Can I do this? I haven't been kissed since before...

His lips meet mine and my eyes flutter closed. Oh god, I missed this feeling. He gently touches his fingers to my face and slides his thumb along my jaw. A thousand pings of sensation flood through me, rushing down my spine, spreading across my skin. His mouth caresses mine, soft but insistent.

Without conscious thought, I shift closer and his other hand slips around my waist. I wasn't expecting the touch, but the feel of his tongue sliding across my lips distracts me from the slight shock. I part my lips, inviting him to deepen the kiss. Breath comes faster, tongues dance. He tastes faintly of wine. I clutch his shirt in tight fists and everything melts away with the heat of his mouth on mine.

His hand slides to the back of my neck and he tightens his grip.

Panic.

I can't move my neck, my head immobilized between his mouth and hand. I open my fists and press hard against his chest, pushing him away from me.

He releases me instantly, his hands dropping. My hands are still on his chest, my arms outstretched.

"I'm sorry," he says. "I shouldn't have done that."

No. *No.* I don't want him to think I didn't want him to kiss me. God, why do I have to be such a disaster? "No, that was... you don't have to apologize."

He's already backing up. Standing. Damn it, he's going to leave.

"Gabriel, please."

He stops.

Deep breath. "That was me, not you. Please don't go."

"Sadie, what's going on?" He lowers himself onto the edge of the couch.

I glance at the ice cream, starting to melt in the carton. Can I tell him? Can I trust him with any of this?

What if he doesn't believe me?

"I'm sorry, this is hard for me," I say. "I moved to Jetty Beach because I had to get away from someone. His name is..." Hard swallow before I can say it out loud. "Adam Cooper. He was causing problems for me. He did some things he shouldn't have and it made me skittish. Too skittish, I think. What he did has nothing to do with you."

"Is that why you have all the locks on the front door?" he asks.

I nod. "It makes me feel safer."

"I'm sorry, I shouldn't have kissed you."

"No, I'm glad you did," I say. "I wanted you to. I'm just not used to it. I got scared for a second."

"You don't have to be afraid of me," he says, his voice so gentle it almost breaks me. He slides his hand over the top of mine, his skin warm. "I won't hurt you. I promise."

I nod. It's all I can do. If I speak again, I'll probably cry.

He takes my hands in his and holds them as he leans in again. He meets my eyes, his eyebrows lifted, our noses on the brink of touching. *Can I?* his eyes say.

I smile and give him another little nod. Keeping his hands clasped with mine, he kisses me again. Soft. Tender. My shoulders relax, the knots of tension easing. His lips are gentle—careful. For the first time in a long time, desire blooms deep in my core.

Gabriel pulls away and meets my eyes. I can see his silent question. *Was that okay?*

I bite my lower lip and smile again.

"I'm going to the farmer's market in the morning. Come with me?"

"Sure," I say, slightly breathless.

He smiles, his eyes crinkling at the corners. "Good. I'll pick you up at nine."

"Okay."

He squeezes my hands before he gets up. There's a part of me that wants him to stay. But somehow, we both seem to know that I can't yet. Even if I *can* imagine him touching me, feeling my bare skin. I can imagine letting him in.

But I'm not ready.

I stand and walk him to the door. "Thank you for coming by."

"I'm very glad I did," he says. "I'll see you in the morning."

"Have a good night, Gabriel."

"I will now." He leans in and brushes the softest of kisses across my lips. "Goodnight."

He leaves and I make sure to secure all the locks. I touch my fingers to my lips, the memory of his mouth against mine branded on them, hot and captivating.

I'm caught in a haze of conflicting emotions. Fear. Longing. Doubt. Tenderness.

Hope.

So much hope in the feel of my swollen lips, my sensitive skin. Hope that maybe I'm not broken beyond repair. Maybe my life didn't end with Adam Cooper.

Maybe it can begin again with Gabriel Parker.

11

SADIE

I'm up early, the excitement of going to the farmer's market with Gabriel making it hard to sleep. The memory of his kiss is still so keen—it could have been seconds ago, not hours. I slept soundly, and despite waking at the crack of dawn, I feel rested.

I shower and get dressed, taking the time to blow-dry my hair so it hangs down in soft waves. I add a touch of makeup, wrinkling my nose at the smattering of freckles across my face.

It's been a while since I checked the email account my family knows about, but I have some time, and I should get it over with. My heart starts to race as I open my laptop and power it on. At first, their emails were full of shouting in all-caps and exclamation points. Demands to know where I am. That I come home. Lots of guilt.

My therapist helped me craft short answers that I could simply copy and paste.

No, I will not tell you where I am, but I'm safe.

No, I am not coming back.

No, I will not give you that information.

She likes me to use the word *no* a lot.

It took a while, but the tone of their emails softened. They stopped demanding things and started asking questions. I still stuck with short replies, not wanting to give them any information that might lead them to my whereabouts. They're my family, and they aren't monsters; but they betrayed me, and I don't think I'll ever trust them again.

I open the account and have three unread emails. The messages from my mother and father—one from each—are expected. The third makes my throat feel like it's closing and a sick feeling rolls through my stomach.

It's from my brother, Tyler.

I read Mom's first. It's an attempt at casual conversation, but I can feel the strain in her words. She tells me she joined a new knitting club. Asks how I am. Do I have a job? She mentions that my cousin is getting married and I'm invited to the wedding.

Yeah, that's a big no.

I send her a short reply, letting her know I do have a job and it's going well. I ignore the casual invite to the wedding.

My dad's message is typical. He hopes I'm okay and says he'll see me soon.

No, you won't, Dad.

I reply with, *I hope you're doing well, too.*

My mouse hovers over my brother's name. Tyler Sedgwick. He hasn't attempted to contact me even once since I left. I have no idea what he thinks about it. All I know is that he stood by his friend when I tried to tell him what Adam did. He didn't believe me. He shook his head and walked away.

I click on his message.

.   .   .

SADIE,

Been a while since we talked. I'd hoped you would have come back by now, but Mom and Dad say you keep insisting that you're not. That's a little extreme, don't you think?

I'm just going to be blunt. This running away thing is bull-shit. You took off and no one knows where you are. What is that about?

Adam isn't mad for what you said about him. Maybe if you just come home, we could all sit down and air this out, once and for all. We all need to move on.

Tyler

I STARE AT THE SCREEN, my mouth hanging open, my heart racing. Adam isn't mad? As if I *care* what Adam is feeling. He could fucking die and I wouldn't shed a single tear.

I close out of email and slam my laptop closed. I'm not even going to dignify that message with a response. Tyler wants to twist this so that I left because I'm afraid that Adam is mad? I hate that he believes that asshole over me—his own sister.

I take a deep breath and count backward from ten, a tool my therapist taught me. By the time I get to one, my heart is resuming its normal rhythm. The sick feeling in my stomach persists, but I know it will pass.

It's not always easy, but one thing I've learned: I'm a survivor. All these tiny little wounds still have the power to sting, but they can't ruin me.

Not again.

It's amazing how much better I feel when Gabriel picks me up. Just seeing him smiling at me when I open the door eases the last vestiges of nausea leftover from reading Tyler's email. I consider talking to Gabriel about it, but decide against it. I'd have to tell him the details of what happened between me and Adam, and I don't think I have the stomach for it. As much as I desperately want to trust him, I'm afraid it might be too much. And I don't want to put a damper on our morning.

Gabriel holds my hand as we wander through the stalls of the market. The sun is warm but a cool breeze comes in off the ocean. He buys us freshly made cinnamon sugar donuts and lattes for breakfast. My heart nearly beats out of my chest when he licks the cinnamon and sugar off my fingertips.

We spend a couple hours walking around, and he chats with a few of the farmers. I love the feel of his hand on my back, or twined together with mine.

When he takes me home, he parks in my driveway and leans in close. What begins as a quick kiss turns into anything but. His mouth caresses mine, his fingertips gently touching my chin. Minutes pass—or maybe time stops, I can't quite tell. My sensitive lips tingle with the heat of his kiss.

Eventually, we pull apart. He walks me to my door and kisses me again before we say goodbye.

Reluctantly, I go inside. But I have to get ready for work soon, and I can't sit in a car making out with Gabriel all day.

Actually, yes I could.

At least I get to see him at work in a couple of hours.

I'm a little nervous when I get to the restaurant. Is Gabriel going to say anything? Are we keeping this quiet? Is there a *this*?

I don't see him when I hang up my purse in the back, so

I get to work. I'm in and out of the kitchen while I help get things ready. He appears, but he's as busy as I am. I see him from behind for a moment, but he's talking to Clover.

Focusing on my job isn't too hard. I like simply being here, knowing he's nearby. There's comfort in his presence. The front doors are opened and our first guests arrive, so I'm quickly occupied with my tables.

I come back into the kitchen and Gabriel's eyes meet mine. His mouth turns up in a subtle smile and a tingle runs through my tummy. I smile back, but my cheeks warm and I glance away as I take my table's appetizers. I feel like everyone here is going to take one look at me and know there's something going on between us. Today at the market it was easy to forget that he's my boss, but it's a complication I can't deny. What are the rest of the staff going to think?

What's Clover going to think?

I can't tell if she notices the way Gabriel keeps looking at me. Of all the people I work with, her opinion of this matters the most to me. She's become the closest thing I have to a friend since I moved, and I hate the idea that she might not like me seeing Gabriel.

I see Clover a little later and she gives me a bright smile. That sets my nerves at ease—just in time for another smoldering look from Gabriel that makes my heart race.

We're busy, and the service goes by quickly. We get things cleaned up for the night and I find myself lingering as the rest of the staff starts to filter out, everyone heading home.

Gabriel is always the last one here. He gives the counters a final wipe down while Sam turns out the dining room lights and leaves. I don't need to stay, and he didn't exactly ask me to. But I can't quite make myself take the final steps to the back door. I fiddle with something in my purse, pretending to search for my keys.

When I glance up, Gabriel is standing in front of me, wearing that quiet smile he shows so rarely in the kitchen.

"I'm glad you're still here," he says.

"Yeah, I at least wanted to say goodnight."

He steps closer and slips a hand on my waist. I tilt my chin up and he leans in, pressing his lips against mine. He's no longer hesitant, like he's waiting to see if I'm willing. He kisses me with purpose, drawing me close to his body, his lips firm. His tongue slides against my lips, beckoning me for more. I give him what he wants, my body softening against him while he kisses me deeply. I drape my arms around his shoulders and lose myself in the feel of kissing him. Strong arms surround me and his mouth is soft and pliant against mine.

Moments pass, and we don't stop, like a couple of teenagers who have a sudden moment unsupervised. One hand reaches beneath my shirt and I gasp at the feel of his hand on the bare skin of my back.

A noise behind me makes us both pause. Gabriel pulls away slightly and his eyes look past me, into the kitchen.

"Don't stop because of me." Clover's voice. "I just forgot my phone. Carry on!"

I feel frozen to the spot, unable to turn around, but I can hear Clover's footsteps as she walks behind me. Gabriel doesn't let go or move away. I follow his eyes as he watches Clover.

"Night, you two," Clover says. "And it's about freaking time, by the way."

Gabriel's shoulders shake with a soft laugh and he rests his forehead against mine.

"Oops," I say. "I guess this isn't a secret anymore?"

He brushes my hair back from my face and rests his palm on my cheek. "You were never going to be a secret."

"I wasn't sure if the rest of the staff would think it's a problem," I say.

"Yeah, I know I'm your boss. But I think it would be worse if we try to hide our relationship."

Relationship? My heart flutters at the sound of that word. "Is that what this is?"

Gabriel's smile disappears and he drops his hand. "If you don't want—"

"Wait." I step closer and put a hand on his chest. "Yes, that's what I want."

His hand rests on the side of my face again. "Good. Me too. Although I feel like making you tag along with me to the market is a poor substitute for a date. We're both working tomorrow, but can I take you out for breakfast?"

Happiness swirls through me like a handful of sparkling confetti. "Yes, I'd love that."

"Good."

He kisses me again, tenacious but unhurried.

"We should probably go home, or I won't be able to let you go," he says, whispering into my mouth.

I nod. As good as this feels, I know I'm not ready for more.

12

GABE

*M*y keys hit my desk with a metallic clink and I sit down. There's a copy of our menu sitting on my desk. I'd bet anything Clover left it there as a reminder that we need to update it. I already added a couple of different dishes from last year, so it won't be exactly the same. But we both know that isn't enough. All it would take is the wrong customer, or worse, a critic, to come in and realize I'm serving the same things for my reputation to take a serious hit.

I thought about spending the morning at home trying some new ideas. But as I sipped my morning coffee, staring at the gourmet kitchen I designed myself, my shoulders slumped. The hollowness that's been eating at me filled my chest. I knew I would only wind up frustrated.

I'm not sure what I need to do to get my spark back. What do people do when the magic runs out? I've been faking it for so long; it's only a matter of time before I can't hide it anymore.

Instead, I called Sadie and took her to lunch. Being with her certainly took the edge off. It always does. I've been spending time with her as often as I can. I have to admit, I'm feeling the strain on my schedule. I'm used to pouring most of my waking hours into the restaurant. Making time for Sadie means I'm falling behind on things at work.

Linda appears at my door. "Afternoon. Have you seen it yet?"

"Have I seen what?"

"The article."

"No, is it out?"

"Yep," she says. "They're sending us the hard copies, so I don't have them yet. But it's up online."

I glance at my laptop, remembering Alice's face when I turned her down. I'm not sure if I want to read it. "Is it good?"

"Yes," she says, emphatic. "It's very positive. It focuses on you being young and living your dream of owning this restaurant, here in your hometown."

"But?" I ask.

"I didn't say *but*."

"I'm sure there's something."

She sighs. "There's a line or two you won't like. It's nothing too bad."

I groan and click the keyboard to bring my laptop out of sleep mode.

"I sent you the link."

"Thanks."

Linda goes back to her office. I open her message and click on the link.

She's right, most of the article isn't bad. The angle Alice chose is of a young man who made his dream come true. How I breathed new life into the restaurant that was so special to me. She uses the story I shared about the old head chef, a tall Italian guy named Nico, and how he'd let me come in and work with him on slow nights when I was a teenager. How my love of cooking blossomed here, in this very kitchen, and how my life came full circle when I took over.

I get toward the end and my back tightens.

Although he cooks delicious food, arguably the best in the region, Gabriel Parker's personal life leaves something to be desired. A self-described workaholic, his addiction to his work keeps him from maintaining close relationships. His wife Amanda left him after he took ownership of the Ocean Mark, unable to cope with the strain his obsession with his career put on their marriage. Now, he spends most of his free time alone, absorbed in his cooking and his business.

I wonder how she found out about Amanda. I don't remember giving Alice her name. She probably asked one of the staff. It figures she'd get in a dig about my relationships—or lack thereof.

Sadie comes to my mind. The feel of her lips. My hands on her soft skin. *Joke's on you, Alice. I'm not nearly as alone as you think.*

As if summoned by my thoughts of her, Sadie appears in my doorway.

"Hey," she says.

Just seeing her face, hearing her voice, is like a balm to my soul. The smile that crosses my face does so without conscious thought. I realize I've been doing a lot more of that lately. "Hi, beautiful."

Her cheeks flush a little and her lips part in a sweet smile. "I heard the article came out. How is it?"

"It's not bad." It's still open on my screen, so I turn the laptop so Sadie can see. I don't know if I've really told Sadie about my ex-wife, so I quickly explain before she can read it. "Listen, I don't think this has come up, but they mention my ex-wife, Amanda. She's been gone for a long time. I haven't seen her in years."

She smiles. "It's okay. We all have stuff in our pasts."

Her eyes move across the screen as she reads. Then she scrolls down, looking at the photographs. I hadn't gotten to those yet. There's a photo of me in the kitchen at the top, but they included more at the end of the article.

Sadie's smile fades and her brow furrows.

"What's wrong?" I ask. Is there something else I didn't read?

"I'm in some of these."

"What?" I spin the laptop around and scroll through the photos. Sure enough, Sadie is in the background in two of the photos—one in the kitchen and one in the dining room. She's not in the foreground, but her face is clearly visible.

Anger burns hot inside me. Sadie asked me not to let them include her in the pictures. I made that very clear. I'd intended to see to it myself, but Alice kept me busy answering questions the entire time they were here, so I didn't see what was being photographed. Damn it, I should have emailed Alice to remind her. But after turning her down, I wanted to avoid talking to her again.

"Sadie, I'm sorry. I told them not to photograph you," I say. "Damn it, I should have had you take that night off so you wouldn't have been here."

A trembling hand covers her mouth and she takes a deep breath.

"I'll call them," I say. "I'll have them pull these pictures. I'm so sorry."

She shakes her head. "No, it's not your fault. And it's probably fine. I'm sorry, I'm sure I'm making a big deal out of nothing."

I wish she would tell me what's going on. Aside from

explaining that she had to move to get away from someone, she hasn't told me why. I haven't pressed her for more. As curious as I am, it doesn't feel right to ask more questions. She'll tell me when she's ready. But there's no mistaking the fear in her eyes, and I'm at a loss for what could have happened that has her so afraid.

"Are you in danger?" I ask.

She takes another deep breath. "I don't think so. It's not like this will be front page news in Missouri. Is my name included?"

I scan through the photos and the captions again. Beneath one it clearly reads, *Servers Sam Martin and Sadie Sedgwick take care of guests in the elegant dining room.*

"Yes," I say. "It does say your name."

She stiffens, her eyes locked on the wall.

"I'm going to call them right now and get them to take these down and remove your name," I say. "It's going to be fine."

She meets my eyes, straightening her back. "Okay. You're right. It will be fine." Another deep breath. "I should get to work. I'll see you out there."

I watch her go, wishing she'd come back and open up. Wishing she'd tell me what happened to her.

She doesn't. Not yet. But I can always see the pain behind her eyes. Feel it in her touch. She's holding onto something that hurt her deeply.

The thought of someone hurting her makes anger bubble up inside again. I'm calling Alice and I'm going to make her take those fucking pictures down. And this time, I don't give two shits about whether I'm being an asshole.

13

SADIE

*T*he running water pours across the plate, rinsing the soap down in a cascade of bubbles. Memories assault me. Things I wish I could forget.

I'M STANDING in the hallway at my parents' house. My back tightens, as if my skin is shrinking over my ribs. The front door closes and I hear voices. Two. Male. Saying hello to my parents. My shoulders slump. Why did Tyler have to bring him?

For a second, I consider feigning a sudden illness as an excuse to go home. The nausea wouldn't be a lie. I feel sick to my stomach—sicker when I hear Adam's laugh.

But I can't let him run me off from my own family. It's just dinner. I can handle him.

With a deep breath, I head into the kitchen to see if my mom needs any help. Luckily, she's the only one there; Tyler and Adam appear to be in the living room with my dad.

"What can I do?" I ask.

Mom bustles about the kitchen, her red and white

checked apron tied around her waist. "The table is set, but you can start bringing the food out."

I grab a bowl of mashed potatoes and take it to the dining room. I glance at the guys, standing nearby. Adam catches my eye and his mouth curls. I look away quickly, breathing through the sick feeling in my stomach.

I wish he didn't make me so uncomfortable. He's my brother's best friend. Hell, my family keeps nudging me toward going out with him. I think my parents always figured he and I would wind up together.

But he's made me feel this way since we were kids. Ever since the night he was sleeping over with Tyler and he came into my room. I couldn't have been more than eleven. He sat on the edge of my bed and told me he wanted to kiss me like a grownup and put his tongue on my privates.

I didn't even understand what that meant, not really. I only knew it scared me. But he told me it was our secret and I was never, ever to tell anyone. He claimed if I did, I'd get in big trouble.

I wish I hadn't believed him. Maybe if I'd spoken up all those years ago, my parents wouldn't have let my brother stay friends with him.

He looks at me again when I walk back toward the kitchen. This time, his tongue flicks out and his upper lip twitches.

God, he's so gross. He's tall and thin, all sinewy muscle. His hands are too big, his fingers oddly long. I get another serving dish from the kitchen and when I come out, he wiggles those fingers at me, facing upward, like he's mimicking something sexual. I glance at Tyler and my dad, but of course Adam did it when they weren't looking. They never see.

I'm silent through dinner, my eyes on my plate. Adam is

seated across from me and I feel his foot nudge mine a few times. I resist the urge to kick him under the table.

Finally, everyone finishes, and my parents get up. My mom starts to clear the table, but Adam stands and takes her dish.

"Here, Mrs. Sedgwick," he says, his voice the epitome of politeness. "I'll clean up. It's the least I can do after this lovely meal."

"Adam, you're such a gentleman," Mom says with a smile. She looks at me. "Sadie can help you. Can't you, dear?"

I don't miss the message in her eyes: she wants me to spend time with Adam. Their once-subtle hints are becoming far less so. It doesn't seem to matter that I just got out of a relationship—one that Adam himself ruined.

But of course, my family took Adam's side. They thought James was overreacting; if he was so threatened by Adam, maybe it was for the best that he broke up with me.

Wordlessly, I get up and start bringing the dishes into the kitchen. I can feel Adam's presence behind me. He sets a stack of plates on the counter and casually brushes his hand across my backside.

I whip around. "Hands to yourself."

He quirks an eyebrow at me. "What?"

"Just back off."

"I'm just doing the dishes here," he says. "You're the one being touchy."

I go back into the dining room to keep clearing the table. Tyler and my parents are out on the back porch. My dad's probably smoking a cigar. I wish they hadn't left me alone with him, although I know they did it on purpose.

Adam is leaning against the counter when I come back

in, my arms full of dishes. His eyes rove down my body; he's making no effort to hide that he's ogling me.

"What?" I ask.

He lifts one shoulder. "Nothing."

"Stop staring at me."

"Why? Don't you enjoy having a man look at you with appreciation?"

"Not particularly," I say, moving past him to set the dishes on the counter.

"Then why do you dress like that?"

I glance down. I'm wearing a silky green tank top and fitted jeans. "What does my outfit have to do with anything?"

"It makes you hard to resist," he says. "Did you pick it for me?"

"No," I say, my voice sharp. "Stop being creepy, Adam. It's not like that. *We're* not like that."

He moves closer, invading my personal space, and leans in to speak quietly in my ear. His breath is hot on my neck, making me shudder.

"Oh, kitten. Someday I'm going to show you. You're going to learn. Soon, kitten. Soon."

I GASP, coming back to reality with a start. I'm standing in *my* kitchen. In Jetty Beach. I'm not in Missouri—not at my parents' house. My hands are clenched around the plate I was rinsing, the water still running. I turn it off and put the plate in the dish dryer.

Deep breaths, Sadie. Deep breaths.

It's been a week since the article came out, and so far, nothing's happened. There's no sign anyone back home saw it. But I'm still on edge.

I check my email every day, always dreading what I might find. I hear from my parents once, and it's the usual. Attempts at conversation, at connection. There's nothing from Tyler. And certainly nothing from Adam.

I'm still wondering how many locks I can fit on my front door.

I head into work, glad for the distraction. And for the knowledge that Gabriel will be there.

Just the thought of seeing him today riles up the butterflies in my tummy. I feel like a kid with a crush. The smile on my face grows the closer I get to the restaurant. It doesn't matter what we're doing—working, hanging out, stealing kisses in his office when we hope no one's looking—he always makes me feel better. Safe. Happy.

I pull up to the Ocean Mark and park in the back. It's such a beautiful place. Tall fir trees give it the ambiance of being set apart from the world. The roar of the ocean carries up the bluff, and the breeze is soft and gentle. The lodge style of the architecture is warm and inviting. It's the kind of place that draws people in from the moment they arrive, making them feel welcome. Cared for.

I love this restaurant. I love it in a way I've never loved a place I've worked before. I *care* about it.

Because it's his. Because he loves it too.

I head inside and hang my purse on a hook in the back. I see Gabriel's office door is half open, and I'm just about to go in and say hi when Clover catches my eye.

"Hey, Sadie," she says with a smile. She rubs her growing belly absently. "Something came for you."

"Really?"

She nods toward a counter in the back where I see a big bouquet of pale pink orchids.

"Are you serious?" I ask. "Those are for me?"

"Yep," she says.

I wander back and eye the flowers. They're lovely, but the sight of them makes me uneasy. Pink orchids used to be my favorite. Did Gabriel send these? Why would he send me flowers at work? And how would he know which ones to send?

There's a card attached to a little plastic stick. I pluck it off and pull it out of the envelope.

Sadie Sedgwick

It doesn't say anything else. No note. No indication who it's from.

A feeling of sickness steals over me. *Oh my god. Please no.*

I turn, ignoring Clover's raised eyebrows, and head straight for Gabriel's office.

Please let these be from him. *Please.*

I knock on his half-open door. "Hey, can I come in?"

"Sure." He's writing something and doesn't look up at me when I slip inside.

There's something about his posture and short reply—and the fact that he's not looking up—that sets me on edge. "Is everything okay?"

"Yeah," he says. "I guess so."

The sick feeling grows. I'm afraid to even ask if he sent the flowers. I already know the answer. "All right."

"You have an admirer or something?" he asks, still not looking.

"The flowers?" I ask.

"Yes, the flowers."

"I guess that means they aren't from you."

His eyes finally lift. "No."

Bile rises in the back of my throat. "Are you sure?"

"Of course I'm sure. I'd know if I sent you flowers." He presses his lips together for a second. "Who did?"

There's a part of me that wants to laugh because I can tell he's trying very hard to hide his jealousy. A vein sticks out in his neck and his face is too still, like he's fighting to keep his expression calm.

But none of this is funny. If Gabriel didn't send those flowers, there's only one other person who could have. Which means...

"Oh my god," I say, putting a hand to my mouth.

"Sadie, is there something you need to tell me?"

There's a hitch in his voice. He thinks I'm seeing someone else behind his back. I don't want him to think that, but I can't seem to say anything. My breath is frozen in my lungs and I can't make myself speak. I put a hand to my chest and try to breathe.

He waits in silence while I collect myself.

"I think it was Adam Cooper," I say, forcing myself to utter his name.

"You mean..." His brow furrows. "You mean the guy you moved to get away from?"

I nod.

"What does the card say?" he asks.

"Nothing." I hold it out for him to see. "Just my name."

He turns the card over. "These could have been ordered online from anywhere."

"Exactly."

"Who is he?" Gabriel asks. "Your ex-boyfriend? Ex-husband?"

"No, he's neither," I say.

Clover peeks her head in behind me. "Hey, chef. We need to get started."

Gabriel nods and Clover disappears back into the kitchen. He stands and walks around his desk, stopping in front of me. He rubs his hands up and down my arms. "Are you okay? Do you want to go home?"

I shake my head. "No, I'd rather be here. It just means... it means he knows where I am."

"I know," he says. "But I need you to listen to me, Sadie. I'm not going to let anything happen to you. I don't care who he is. Whatever you're worried about, it won't happen."

His strong hands on my arms and quiet voice shore me up, fill me with confidence.

"Do you want me to throw them away?" he asks.

"Yes, please do." I pause, chewing on my lip. "Did you think there was someone else?"

"I was a little worried about that, yeah," he says. "I didn't know why you'd be getting flowers at work. I know it's not your birthday, and you said your parents don't know where you live. I thought maybe—"

"No," I say, reaching up to touch a finger to his lips. "I swear to you, Gabriel, I'm not hiding something like that from you."

He leans his forehead against mine. "I should have just asked."

I can't help the smile that crosses my lips. "Were you jealous?"

He kisses my forehead. "What can I say? I want you all to myself."

"You have me all to yourself," I say.

Unless my drama is too much. Unless I stop being worth the trouble.

14

GABE

*T*oss the flowers into the dumpster outside and brush my hands together. When the delivery guy brought them in for Sadie, I was hit with surge of anger. Jealousy. Who the fuck was sending *my* woman flowers at work? I certainly didn't send them.

I admit I looked at the card. Nothing on it but her name.

It didn't occur to me that they could be from that Adam guy, whoever he is. I wish she would just tell me what happened. What made her pack up her life and run? I don't know if she still talks to her family, or if they know where she is. I don't know why she left—not really. It must have been something terrible. People don't usually leave and worry about keeping hidden over something small.

So what the fuck did this douchebag do to her? She said he's not an ex. What could he have done that has her running? Has her so scared?

I'm afraid I know, but I can't bring myself to even think it.

And I don't understand why she doesn't trust me enough to tell me the truth.

Sadie seems calm and collected throughout the dinner service. I catch her eye and smile as often as I can—mostly because I like seeing her smile back at me. I like making the light in her eyes shine. I like the feeling that when she's with me, she's not so sad, even if we're just working together.

But she's holding back from me, in more ways than one. It doesn't seem to matter how much her body melts for me when I kiss her. There's a wall she won't let me through. I've never pushed her—in fact, I've never even suggested we take things to the next level. I've wanted to invite her back to my place, or suggest we go to hers. But there's an invisible barrier that I can feel between us. I'm not sure how to get past it, and I'm worried about scaring her off if I try too hard.

But I have to admit, I'm getting impatient.

I'm fine with taking a relationship slow, but god, I want her so bad it hurts. The little taste I've gotten has me positively addicted. Kissing her goodnight, little brushes of skin against my fingers, they're not enough. I want more of her. I want all of her.

I'm just not sure how to get through.

At the end of the night, when everyone is gathering their things and leaving, Sadie waits for me. She always does. I love to see her hesitating in the back, pretending to look for something in her purse. Like she needs an excuse to stay.

I think it's time I stop standing on the other side of her wall, and see if there's a door she'll let me through.

"How you doing?" I pick up her hand and kiss it. "Tired?"

"A little," she says. "My feet hurt."

"Yeah, it was busy tonight." I pause and kiss her fingers again. "What would you think about coming home with me tonight?"

Her eyes widen and her lips part. I keep hold of her hand, rubbing the backs of her knuckles with my thumb.

"I'm not sure."

"There's no pressure for anything if you do," I say, and I mean it. "I'm just not ready to let you go tonight."

She nods. "Okay."

"Good." I lean in and brush my lips against hers. It's tempting to grab her and press her body against me, but my gut is telling me to be careful. So I listen.

I offer to drive her—we can leave her car at the restaurant—but she insists on driving herself. We get to my place and she parks her car next to mine.

It's where Amanda used to park, and the feeling I get seeing Sadie's car there is not lost on me. I like it.

I like it a lot.

She seems nervous when I walk her up to my front door. I rub slow circles on her lower back. She comes in with me and puts her things down. I tell her to make herself comfortable on the couch while I go into the kitchen.

"Wine?" I ask.

"Yeah, that would be great."

I open a nice bottle of red and pour. We sit on my couch, facing each other, and sip our wine. Sadie's legs are tucked up beneath her. I rest a hand on her thigh and trace little circles with my thumb. We chat for a while and she seems to relax.

She sets her empty wine glass down. I lean in and touch her face, running my fingers along her jaw. She's so delicate. Tilting my face, I connect my mouth to hers, pressing my lips in a soft kiss. My hand moves back, threading my fingers through her silky hair.

She sucks in a breath and pulls away.

I drop my hand. "Are you okay?"

"Yes," she says. "No. I don't know."

I lick my lips and avoid her gaze. Why does she do this? Why does she pull away? "Sadie, if you didn't want to come tonight, it's okay. You can go home."

She bites her lower lip and looks away. "No, that's not it."

"Then what is it?" I ask. "What's happening here? If you're not ready for this, it's all right. I like you. A lot. I'm not some twenty-one-year-old douchebag who just wants to get in your pants. I'm way past that at this point in my life."

"No, I know you aren't," she says. "And I like you too. So much. That's why this is so hard."

"You need to tell me the truth." I take a breath. "Sadie, who is Adam Cooper?"

She wrings her hands together in her lap, watching them. "Okay." Deep breath. "He was my brother Tyler's best friend. Still is, I guess. We all grew up together. My parents treated him like another son. When we were kids it was usually fine, but as we got older, he started to make me uncomfortable. He never did anything when other people could see. But he'd catch me alone and whisper things, or try to touch me. He'd walk in on me in my room and pretend it was an accident, things like that. My family thought he was great, but he was so different when people were watching.

"I went away to college and didn't see him for a long time. After college, I moved back to my hometown. He had moved away, so it wasn't a big deal. But then he moved back. One night, I was at my parents' house and he showed up with Tyler. He was polite in front of my family, but he kept looking at me. It made me sick the way it used to when we were younger."

She pauses and shifts a little, but I stay silent, waiting.

"After that, he started showing up everywhere," she says.

"He'd come to my work. He got my number from Tyler and started texting me constantly. I'd see him when I was out shopping or running errands, and I realized he was following me around. I tried to tell Tyler that Adam was getting weird, but he didn't believe me."

She stops and stares at her hands for a long moment. I have a feeling I know where this is going. My heart rate speeds up and a hot ember of anger smolders in my gut.

"It got worse. Adam started showing up at my house, sometimes in the middle of the night. He'd leave notes on my car, or slip them under my front door. Some of them were lines from books or movies, but most just said *you're mine*. He always knew where I was, no matter what I did. I was dating a guy named James at the time and Adam started texting him, telling him that I was sleeping with Adam behind his back. I tried to tell James that Adam was crazy, but eventually he decided I wasn't worth the hassle."

"After James broke up with me, Adam got worse," she continues. "He started sending me pictures of women, usually tied up and gagged. He left a vase of dead flowers on my porch. He called my boss and tried to get me fired. I should have told someone, but it all seemed so insane. Who would believe me? I couldn't prove it was Adam. The only thing I could prove was that he'd been texting James, but that could have been chalked up to jealousy—a guy trying to chase my boyfriend away. Adam admitted that he liked me, and my family was encouraging me to give him a chance and go out with him. They were mad at me for constantly turning him down."

"Then one night, he came over, late. He was banging on my door and I wouldn't let him in. I thought about calling the police, but I didn't. I should have. But I didn't think he'd actually hurt me. I thought he'd get tired of it and go home."

She stops again and I'm almost afraid to let her continue. I know what she's going to say. I hold still, my body tense, the burning coal of anger growing hotter with every word.

"I made the biggest mistake of my entire life that night. I opened the door for him. I thought if I let him in and talked to him, I could tell him to go home and he'd leave." Another deep breath, and when she continues, her voice is shaky. "He didn't. He pushed his way in. He said I was his and no one else was ever going to have me. That I'd been his since we were kids. And he was tired of waiting for me."

I clench my teeth together and ball my hands into fists.

"I tried to fight him off, but he was so strong. And I was so shocked. I couldn't believe what was happening at first, and by the time it really sank in what he was doing, it was too late. He bent me over my dining table and ripped my pants down."

Breath comes faster, my chest rising and falling rapidly.

"I couldn't stop him. I screamed at him to stop, and he wouldn't listen. I don't want to tell you all the things he did. When it was over, he just left. I didn't know what to do. I went to my room and curled up in a ball and cried all night. I was in so much pain and so scared. The next morning, I decided to go to the hospital. I wasn't sure what they would do, but I couldn't lie at home doing nothing. I told them what happened and they called the police. I told the police everything. Every bit of it. And then I called my parents."

A red haze colors the edges of my vision. I stay calm on the outside. On the inside, I'm a storm.

"My parents took me home and sat in my living room with me. My dad was pacing up and down the floor. And they told me I had to drop the charges." She sniffs and swipes a hand beneath her eyes. "They didn't believe me.

They couldn't fathom that Adam Cooper, the boy who had practically grown up at our house, could have done such a thing. They said I must have done something to lead him to believe that I wanted to sleep with him. They said I was awful for throwing out such a hateful accusation."

She covers her mouth with her hand and looks away. I think she might be done, but I don't know what to say. Then she drops her hand and meets my eyes. They're shining green, flinty with anger and pain.

"It got worse when Tyler found out. He yelled at me, saying I'd ruined Adam's life. How could I do something so horrible to another person?" She's breathing as hard as I am and her jaw sets in a firm line. "They thought I lied, Gabriel. They thought I slept with Adam, and then he rejected me, so I made up a story about him raping me."

"I let them bully me into dropping the charges," she continues, and I see her fighting with her rage. "One of the police officers came over to my house to try to talk me out of it. But it was my word against Adam's, and I didn't have much of a case. Adam didn't deny we'd slept together, so the physical evidence the hospital took hardly mattered. He said it was consensual, and that we had a fight afterward. He painted me as a spoiled little girl who had been harboring a crush on her big brother's friend since she was a kid. He implied that I pushed him into sleeping with me."

"So I gave up," she says, her anger melting away, her tone full of defeat. "My parents wouldn't stand behind me. My brother stopped speaking to me. I didn't have anyone who believed me. Adam acted like the victim, like I'd ruined his life by accusing him of rape. We lived in a small town, so everyone heard. People watched me when I went out, looking at me like I was the one who had done something wrong."

"I didn't hear anything from Adam for a while," she continues. "I thought maybe things would die down and I could go back to my life. But then I saw him when I stopped to get gas. And again at the grocery store. He left a note on my car. I saw him drive by my house. I got more pictures in the mail and left on my doorstep—pictures where the women looked dead or hurt, always tied up. I realized he was never going to leave me alone. And next time, it was going to be worse."

I finally manage to ask a question. "Is that when you left?"

She nods. "When he started stalking me again—because no matter what my parents say, that's exactly what he was doing—I knew I'd never be safe if he could find me. So I made plans. I packed what I could carry, sold my car, dumped my cell phone, and paid some lady to buy a bus ticket for me. I changed buses several times in different cities. I actually didn't know where I'd go. I just kept riding. Paying cash for cheap hotels. I stayed in different places for a few weeks at a time. I even got a job in some small town in Idaho, but I decided not to stay. Eventually, I made it all the way out here."

"No one believed me," she says, her voice so quiet. "He tortured me, harassed me, stalked me, and raped me. My own family—the people who should have stood by me—took his side. They said I ruined his life. But he ruined mine. He ruined *me*."

My hands shake with rage and I'm not sure I trust myself to speak again. My chest feels like it's been ripped in half, my heart crushed under the weight of her pain. I'm second-guessing everything I've ever said to her. Every time I've touched her. Have I pushed her too hard? Have I scared her?

Does she see him when we're together? Is she afraid I'll do the same?

I literally want to kill this guy. I want to find him and wrap my hands around his throat and squeeze until his fucking face turns purple. I want to choke the life out of him so he pays for what he did to Sadie. So he'll know, in his final, agonizing moments, what real pain is.

And then he'll be gone, and he'll never hurt my Sadie again.

"Gabriel?" she says, her voice trembling. "Please say something."

I reach out and scoop her into my arms, drawing her close. Rage pours through my veins. Not only did he violate her in the worst way, her family betrayed her. Left her on her own. I think about my own family, the people closest to me. I know, deep in my soul, that if I was in trouble, they'd stand by me. Hell, I have more than just my relatives. I have Clover, and the entire Jacobsen family. I have Finn and Lucas. They might be goofballs, but they're loyal. They'd have my back if I ever needed them.

Sadie has no one. She was wounded and left for dead, like an animal on the side of the road.

I won't let that stand. There isn't anything I can do to change what happened to her, but I can sure as shit change what happens now.

I move back and cup her face gently in my hands. "I want you to listen to me. I believe you. I would never doubt you, and I know this is real. And this is important, baby. Hear my voice. I will *never* hurt you. And I will never, ever let something like that happen to you. It doesn't matter if he finds you. It doesn't matter what he does. I'll keep you safe. I swear it."

15

GABE

I wake up with Sadie in my arms.

I couldn't bear to let her go last night. We were both exhausted, and after a little coaxing, I convinced her to stay with me.

Yes, having this sexy-as-hell woman sleeping next to me in just one of my t-shirts and a pair of my boxers was a little torturous. But it was blissful torture. I gave her space, keeping to one side of the bed. But sometime in the night, I woke up with her snuggled up against me. Careful so I wouldn't wake her, I tucked her into my arms. The scent of her in my bed and her body curled up next to mine were like heaven. I settled in with her, feeling more whole than I have in a long time.

Maybe more whole than I've ever felt.

Hearing what she's been through—hearing the dreaded word *rape*—almost tore me in two. A part of me suspected. But listening to her tell her story, it was worse than I thought.

She thinks this broke her—that he broke her. But she

doesn't see her strength. She's so strong to have survived everything she's been through.

I hear her deep breath, feel her begin to stretch languidly as she wakes. It's not the first time we've woken up together in the same bed, but this time, everything feels different.

She finally let me in.

"Morning," I say, placing a kiss on her nose when she looks over her shoulder at me.

"Good morning."

I trace my fingers along the bit of exposed skin between her shirt and shorts. I wish I wasn't wearing sweatpants—I want to feel her bare legs against mine.

She nuzzles into me while I trail kisses along her neck and shoulder. I slide my hand beneath her shirt, touching the smooth skin of her taut belly, up her ribcage, beneath her breast. I kiss her neck again, just behind her ear. "Is this okay?"

She nods and her back arches, her ass pressing against my erection. I run my hand down to her hip and grip it, firm but gentle, and press my cock against her.

Her body stiffens and immediately, I back off. I actually have no idea how to navigate this without hurting her. I already know I'm never going to push her into doing something she doesn't want. I'll be the most patient guy on the fucking planet for her. But if I never try, we won't ever see where this can go.

"Sorry," I whisper. "I won't push you, baby. You just feel so good."

She turns so she's facing me, and tucks her hands beneath her cheek. "You feel good too. So good. I didn't think a man could make me feel like you do. But I'm still not sure I can do this."

I reach out and brush the hair back from her face. "Then we take it slow. We figure this out together."

"Are you sure?" she asks.

"Positive." I get an idea, and I wonder how she'll feel about it. "What if we try something?"

"Try what?" she asks.

"What if you're completely in charge," I say. "I'll promise not to do anything unless you tell me to. I won't touch you, or even move unless you tell me. You can take it as far as you want, stop whenever you want."

"So you'll just lie here?" she asks.

"Exactly."

"But I can touch you?"

I take a deep breath. "Sadie, you can do anything you want to me. If you want to try this, you're in complete control from this moment on. I won't do anything unless you tell me to."

Her eyes take me in for a long moment, like she's considering whether this might work. She licks her lips and touches my chest through my shirt. I'm already hard, and the feel of her hand on me—and the knowledge that I can't do anything to her—makes my groin ache.

But I can do this for her.

She grabs the bottom of my shirt and lifts. I sit partway up and let her take it off me, only moving enough to be cooperative. I prop myself up on my elbows while her eyes rove down my chest, my abs, to the hard bulge in my sweats. She chews on her bottom lip and looks me up and down again, sending out a tentative hand to touch my chest. Her fingers are warm against my skin.

"Lie down," she whispers.

I lean back, letting my head hit the pillow, and nudge the

covers down with my feet. Sadie's fingers whisper through my chest hair, her touch leaving a trail of heat.

Two hands touch me and I work to keep my breathing even. She slides her fingers down to the waistband of my sweats and I swallow hard.

"Can I?" she asks, her fingers tentative over the waistband.

"I told you, baby," I say. "Anything."

She lowers them down my legs slowly, and the act of her undressing me only makes my cock harder. I lift my hips so she can pull my pants off, then lie still.

I watch her trail her fingers up and down my thighs, her auburn hair falling loose around her shoulders. I glance down at her breasts, see her nipples poking through her t-shirt, and quickly look at the ceiling. I don't need visuals to make this harder.

She runs her hands up my legs and past my cock. Involuntarily, I twitch, and she pulls her hands away.

"Sorry," I say.

"It's okay."

She keeps touching me, exploring my body with her fingertips, her caress light. At first, she seems wary, her movements tense and halting.

I hear her deep intake of breath and she spreads her hands, pressing her palms into my chest. The increased contact and pressure has me groaning, a low sound in the back of my throat. It's taking every ounce of willpower I have to keep my hands at my sides.

She leans her face next to mine, brushing the side of her cheek against my jaw. I'd love to thread my hands through her hair, take her mouth in a kiss. But I don't. I lie as still as I can, riding out the slow torture of her skin against mine.

Her lips press against my neck. I ball my hands into fists

and my dick strains against my underwear, the tip peeking out the top. The jasmine scent of her hair fills my nose.

She kisses down my chest and another low groan escapes my throat. Her mouth feels so good. I resist the urge to touch her—to slide my hand up her ribcage and cup her breast. She goes lower and I groan again. I don't know how she's doing this, but I'm on fire, my cock uncomfortably hard.

Our eyes meet and she licks her lips. "You still won't move?"

"Not until you say otherwise."

"What if I do this?" She throws one leg over me and straddles my thighs, my aching cock in front of her.

"You're in control, baby."

"Can I do this?" She pulls up on the hem of her t-shirt.

I nod and she pulls it over her head, revealing full tits and perfect pink nipples. Oh fuck. My balls clench and I squeeze my eyes shut.

"What's wrong?" she asks.

I take a deep breath before answering. I'm on the verge of losing control and she hasn't even touched my cock. "God, Sadie, you're so fucking beautiful. I don't know if I can look at you like this without coming all over myself."

Her thighs clench around my legs and I hear her gasp. Hands trace the waistband of my underwear and I clamp my teeth together.

"Baby, one wrong move and I'm going to come," I say, my eyes still closed.

Her voice is soft and she pulls down my underwear, freeing my cock. "What if I want you to?"

I take a ragged breath. "I told you, you can do whatever you want. I'm just warning you."

"Look at me," she says.

I open my eyes and stare at her. Bright green eyes stare back and she bites down on her lower lip, her hands resting on my lower abdomen. She looks down at my cock and I follow her gaze. A bead of moisture glistens on the tip.

She shifts her position, moving up my legs so the apex of her thighs rests just below my balls. I groan and close my eyes again, clenching my fists.

"Do you hate this?" she whispers.

"No."

She rolls her hips forward, almost pressing her pussy against my cock. "I want to, Gabriel, but I don't think I can yet."

"It's okay, baby. You don't have to do anything you don't want to do."

"What would you do if I had to stop now?" she asks.

"To you? Nothing," I say. "But I'd need a few minutes in the bathroom."

"Why won't you look at me?" she asks.

I realize my eyes are closed again. I open them and meet her gaze. "I'm trying to stay in control and it's really fucking hard when I look at you."

"Will you tell me what you want to do to me?" she asks.

"Are you sure?" I ask.

She nods, biting down on her lower lip, her hands resting on my abs. "I want you to tell me. I need to hear it."

"I want to take off your shorts. Then I'd use my fingers to touch you, caress you, help you relax. I'd play with you to make you wet—make you want my cock inside you."

"Then what?"

"Then I'd lick my fingers to taste you."

She gasps and her thighs flex against my legs again.

"I'd roll you onto your back and very slowly push my

cock into your wet pussy. And baby, I'd enjoy every aching second of that first thrust."

She shifts her hips again and my balls tighten.

"Fuck, Sadie." My breath quickens and my heart beats hard. "I'd fuck you like no one has ever fucked you before. I'd kiss you everywhere while I plunge my cock into you. Your face. Your lips. I'd suck on those gorgeous nipples and drive us both crazy."

My cock aches so badly if she so much as touches me, I'm going to explode.

"What else?" she whispers, her voice full of urgency.

"I'd fuck you until you're calling my name, until your pussy is so hot you can't think. Your pussy would clench around my cock, and you'd come so hard you won't know where you are."

"Oh, god," she says.

"Then I'd unload in you," I say. "I'd come in you, and the feel of my cock pulsing inside you would make you come again."

A soft moan escapes her lips and she shifts her hips forward again, rubbing her pussy against my cock.

"Oh fuck, Sadie," I growl.

She leans forward, letting her tits hit my chest, her hands on either side of me. She rubs against me again and my balls draw up tight. I grip the sheets, my fingers clenching around the fabric.

My words are strangled; I can barely get them out. "I'm gonna come if you do that again."

Two quick thrusts of her hips and her hot pussy strokes across my massively sensitive cock. My eyes roll back, my back tightens, and I unleash. Come spurts hot between our bodies. I growl with every pulse. She keeps moving, her erect nipples dragging across my skin, the heat of her pussy rubbing on my cock, so good even through her clothes. I groan again, the waves of my orgasm rolling through me.

It finally subsides and Sadie collapses on top of me. Her breath is warm against my neck, her body draped across mine.

I'm not sure if she wants me to move yet, but the desire to hold her is too much. Tentatively, I wrap my arms around her and hold her close. She stays relaxed, so I keep her in my arms and close my eyes, breathing her in, reveling in the release she gave me.

After long moments, she sits up, straddling my hips, and I drop my arms to my sides.

"Thank you," she says.

I'm glad she feels good about this, but I hate that she got me off and I didn't do anything for her. "Do you want anything else?"

"Like what?"

"Do you want me to make you feel good?"

"You already did," she says.

"Not good enough," I say.

"I don't know if I can anymore," she says.

"You don't know if you can come?" I ask.

She shakes her head.

I gently caress her thighs. "Maybe you can let me try someday."

She gives me a shy smile and nods. "I'm sorry if this was too much."

"Baby, you don't need to apologize," I say. "I wanted to do this for you."

She glances down at her stomach, then mine, both sticky with my come. "I didn't think that would happen."

"I don't think I can help it with you," I say.

"Can I tell you something?"

"Of course."

She chews on her lip before answering. "It felt good when you came on me."

I squeeze her legs again. "That felt incredible. I hope you'll let me do more someday. I want to do that inside you."

"I want that too," she says, her voice quiet.

Her words hit me in the chest and squeeze my heart. I can see how wounded she is. On the outside, she's perfect—beautiful and unblemished. But on the inside, she's been torn to shreds.

"Don't be afraid," I say. "If you want to do this again, we can. But you don't have to make me come. You don't owe me anything. We can do whatever you need so you feel comfortable. So you feel safe with me."

She takes a shuddering breath and a tear slides down her cheek. "Thank you. I don't know what I did to deserve you, but you're the most amazing man I've ever met."

I push myself up and shift so I'm sitting with Sadie in my lap. I wrap my arms around her and hold her close. Her arms fold around my neck and I feel her take deep breaths, her breasts pressing against my chest. Her skin feels so good. I could sit with her like this all day.

She pulls away and looks down. "Maybe we should clean up."

"Yeah, I suppose you're right."

She touches my face, her hand caressing my jaw. "Will you shower with me?"

"Of course, if you want me to."

"Yes, I do."

I lean in and kiss her lips softly, keeping my grip on her light so she knows I'll let go if she needs me to. We get up and go into the bathroom, stripping off the last of our clothes and letting them fall to the floor. I'm sated, but my cock reacts to the sight of her exquisite body. Her round breasts. The soft curve of her waist into her hips. Her toned thighs.

She glances down at my cock and raises her eyebrows. "Are we sure I'm safe to shower with him?"

I laugh. "This is what happens when you're so damn sexy. But yes, of course you're safe."

We get in and rinse off under the warm water. I turn her gently so her back faces the spray and wash her hair, running my fingers along her scalp. When we're both rinsed off, she turns and without a word, wraps her arms around me. She presses her naked body against mine and I feel the soft trembling in her shoulders as she cries.

I hold her beneath the warm water, my chest aching. She splits my heart in two, the edges ragged and bleeding. Suddenly, I know something with every fiber of my being.

I'll do *anything* to help her heal.

16

GABE

The kitchen is quiet in the early morning. Linda is the only other one here, and her office is upstairs. Technically, I'm not supposed to be here. It's my day off. But I'm having an issue with one of our suppliers, and I figured I'd come in and see if I can deal with it.

Of course, I don't *need* to do this today. This issue isn't pressing. I could deal with it later in the week. But I woke up this morning—alone, because Sadie didn't stay over last night—and I was restless. I used to draw on that pent-up energy and use it in my cooking. But I didn't even want to *look* at my kitchen today.

My phone dings with a text. It's from Sadie.

Sadie: Morning, sexy.

Me: Hi, beautiful. Sleep well?

Sadie: More or less. You?

Me: Sort of. I missed you.

Sadie: Me too. Do you have anything going on today? We're both off until Wednesday.

It's true, we are both off on the same days. That's not a coincidence. I made sure Sadie and I have the same schedule. One of the perks of being the boss, I guess. I was planning to text her after I got some work done; I wasn't sure she'd be up this early.

Me: Just getting a few things done at the restaurant. Then I'm free. Have something in mind?

Sadie: You're at work?

Me: Yeah. But I'd love to see you today.

Sadie: Okay. Text me when you're done?

Me: Will do.

I almost add something else, and the words are already typed before I realize what I'm saying. I quickly backspace, deleting it. It felt so natural to end with it. To say *Love you.*

I'm glad I caught myself. We haven't said those words to each other, and the first time can't be in a stupid text message. Although it says something that it came so easily.

Probably because it's true.

I do love her. I love her like crazy. And it's not even something that scares me. I guess I'm pretty far beyond being a guy afraid of commitment—afraid of what it means to utter those words to someone else. Of course, I've kind of been there, done that, and it didn't work out so well for me.

But Sadie is different. It doesn't matter what she's running from, or what she has in her past. I want to be her future.

I turn my attention back to work. The sooner I get done, the sooner I can be with her. I search through some scanned documents, looking for the agreement with the supplier. It reminds me of some other issues Linda sent that I need to see to. This isn't my favorite part of business ownership, but it has to be done.

"Hey."

Sadie's voice jolts me from concentration.

"Hey," I say, furrowing my brow. She's standing in my

office doorway, dressed in light blue shirt and khaki capris, a pair of strappy sandals on her feet. "How did you get here so fast?"

She shrugs. "I don't think I did. I texted you half an hour ago."

"Did you?" I ask. "I guess I wasn't paying attention to the time."

"I have an idea," she says. There's energy in her voice. Excitement. Her green eyes sparkle and the corners of her lips twitch in a mischievous smile.

"Yeah?"

"Let's go out of town," she says.

I shrug. "Sure. When?"

"Now."

"Now?" I ask. "As in, right now?"

"Yes," she says. "We don't have to go far. But you need a couple of real days off, and I think the only way to keep you from coming in here is to get you out of town."

I open my mouth to argue, but it's hard to deny that she's right when I'm sitting at my desk on my day off.

"Please," she says, clasping her hands together in a mimicry of begging.

Like I could deny this woman anything.

"Okay," I say. "Where do you want to go?"

"I don't know," she says. "Actually, I thought I'd have a harder time convincing you. I didn't think past how I was going to get you to agree. Emma said I'd have better luck amputating your arm than pulling you away from work for two days."

I laugh and shake my head. "Sounds like something my sister would say." I pause for a moment, considering. "You know what? A friend of mine has a cabin that's a couple hours from here. He told me I can use it anytime, but I've never taken him up on it. Let me text him and see if it's free."

"That sounds perfect," she says.

I fire off a text to my friend Joe and much to my surprise, he answers immediately. The cabin is free, and I'm more than welcome to use it. He sends me the code for the door, and tells me to have a great time.

"Wow," I say. "That was easy. I guess we're on."

"Maybe it was fate," she says.

"Now you sound like Clover."

An hour later, we're on the road, bags in the back. It's about a two-hour drive. We pull up the long driveway to the cabin, nestled back in the woods. It's built of logs, so the outside looks rustic. The inside is anything but.

"This place is incredible," Sadie says, turning in a slow circle after she walks in.

The ceiling is exposed wood beams, and the furniture is all sleek brown leather. There's a bedroom and bathroom on the back side, but the showpiece of the cabin—if 'cabin' is even the word—is the kitchen.

"My friend Joe is a chef," I say. "A talented one, I might add. He lives in L.A., but he likes coming up here to get away from it all. So of course, his kitchen is incredible."

Everything is top of the line. Stainless steel. Enormous fridge with a pull-out freezer. Six-burner, state-of-the-art gas stove with a grill. Fully stocked pantry. Every pot, pan, dish and utensil a chef could ever need.

We get settled, putting our bags in the bedroom. The kitchen has staples, but nothing perishable, so we decide to go into the nearby town. There's a grocery store and an open-air market just across the street. We stop at the market first and take our time, wandering through the stalls.

The scents fill my nose—cedar, lavender, and the sweet

tang of freshly picked berries. I pause in front of a stall with baskets of vegetables. The sugar snap peas catch my eye. How could I use those? Sautéed. No, blanched in lightly salted water. The color red is in my mind—red like Sadie's hair. It makes me think of red chili. My mind keeps going. Korean gochujang. Rice vinegar. Flank steak. I can taste the heat on my tongue. Feel the crunch of vegetables. It's starting to come together.

I move through the market with purpose now, Sadie following along behind. The colors and textures start speaking to me. I can feel the flavors in my mouth—not taste them, *feel* them. I know what I need and I go through both the market and the neighboring store until I'm sure I have everything.

"You don't have to cook tonight," Sadie says as I gather my ingredients on the huge island back at the cabin.

"I know." I'm distracted, so I force myself to meet her eyes. "Sorry, I just... I have an idea. It's hard to explain."

I start preparing everything. Mix the marinade. Score the steak. It needs to rest a while, so I put it aside while I start chopping vegetables.

Sadie watches, asking an occasional question. Although the kitchen isn't familiar, I move around as if I've been using it for years. Ideas come to me, tastes and textures combining.

Throughout it all, I keep one goal in mind. Making something Sadie will love. I've never cooked for her—not really. Not like this. Not with the frenzy of inspiration thrumming through me, guiding my hands. It's been so long since I felt this way. So long since I felt anything when I'm cooking. This burst of energy is so familiar. The rush of creating.

I thought I might have lost this.

I relax as I work, and chat more with Sadie. I open a bottle of wine while I sear the steak. My mind feels so clear, the flavors coming together just as I thought they would.

This is food for me. It's so much more than nutrition. More than any individual ingredient or taste. It's the way the pieces come together. The textures. The spices. The flavors and colors. It all creates an experience. I can visualize the end in my mind as I work. I can see what it's going to look like on the plate. What it's going to feel like in the mouth. Every bite.

And I know what I want Sadie to feel when she eats it. I want her to know what I feel for her. If I can't love her with my body the way I want to, I can love her with this. With the work of my hands. With something I make for her. It's a small thing—it won't do my feelings justice—but this means a lot to me.

When everything is ready, I send Sadie out to the dining table so I can plate it without her watching.

It's a steak salad with roasted peanuts and red chili dressing. Tender slices of medium rare steak sit on a bed of butter lettuce, sugar snap peas, Persian cucumbers, radishes, and scallions. The dressing has just enough heat to stimulate the tongue without burning. The crisp vegetables compliment the juicy steak perfectly. The peanuts add crunch.

It looks beautiful on the simple white dishes. Exactly like I pictured it in my mind.

I slide the plate in front of Sadie, a little thrill of nerves running through me.

"This looks amazing." She leans in to take in the aromas. "It smells so good."

I watch her with anticipation as she takes her first bite.

She tests it, tasting it thoroughly, as if she knows this matters to me.

Her eyes drift closed and she hums with pleasure. "Oh, Gabriel. This is incredible."

"You like it?"

"I love it," she says. "The steak is so tender, it literally melts in my mouth. There's a kick that doesn't hit right away. It burns just the right amount. My mouth is warm, but not like I need to douse myself with water. And there's a crunch —the crispness of the vegetables, and those roasted peanuts. It all works together perfectly."

My chest swells with pride. I watch her take another bite and she lets out another soft moan. I'm not sure if I'm going to eat mine or just watch Sadie enjoy her dinner. I'm a little buzzed on the feeling of creativity. Of providing her with the exact experience I set out to create.

I trusted my instincts, and it worked. I can't even remember the last time that happened.

"You need to try this," she says between bites. "It's like heaven in my mouth."

"I'm really glad you like it," I say. I taste a bite and I'm pleased with the outcome. She's right, the steak is perfectly tender, and the heat of the dressing is spot on. The flavors and textures complement each other well.

It's not fancy, but it felt good to make it. And it feels even better to watch Sadie enjoy it.

"Is this how you come up with new recipes for the restaurant?" she asks between bites.

"Actually, yes," I say. "Sort of. I didn't make this with that in mind. But I used to do a lot of experimenting, both at home and at the Mark."

"What did you have in mind when you made this, then?"

"You."

She pauses, her fork halfway to her mouth. "Me?"

"Yes, you. I saw those snap peas and they looked so crisp and fresh. And your hair makes me think of spice. Of heat. So a red chili marinade and dressing. And the rest came to me. It's been a while since I felt so inspired." I put my fork down and hold her gaze. "Mostly, though, I wanted to make you something you'd enjoy."

"You've done that," she says. "No question."

I smile, brimming with satisfaction. We finish our meal and Sadie eats every bite. I didn't plan dessert, but I easily whip up a simple chocolate custard. We sit on the couch together and dip fresh strawberries in the silky chocolate, feeding them to each other, while we finish off our bottle of cabernet.

Sadie settles in next to me and I feel a deep sense of contentment that I haven't felt in a long time.

17

SADIE

I think I just ate the best meal I've ever had in my entire life. It was fresh, spicy, tender—absolutely delicious.

Watching Gabriel cook was fascinating. He made it look effortless. His deft hands sliced, chopped, grilled, and tossed the ingredients with expert care. There was something in his eyes while he was working—something I haven't seen before. A spark of excitement. Of passion. He doesn't usually look that way when he's cooking—at least not that I've noticed. I wonder what's different tonight.

Maybe it's being away from the pressures of work. But I'd love to believe it has something to do with me.

And the dessert that he just threw together? He said he wanted something sweet, and fifteen minutes later, he produced the most decadent chocolate custard I've ever tasted. It was silky smooth on my tongue, with a rich chocolate flavor that complimented the sweetness of the fresh strawberries we picked up at the market.

A small fire crackles in the fireplace, more for the ambiance than the heat. We're sitting shoulder to shoulder on the couch, our feet propped up on the small table in front of us, toes pointing toward the flames. My belly is full and my eyes are drowsy in the aftermath of the delicious meal.

"Sorry," I say after a long silence. "The food made me sleepy."

"Don't apologize," Gabriel says, his voice soft. "This is nice."

Nice. It is nice, that's true. But I wish I could handle more than *nice.*

My mind drifts to the other day, when he let me touch him. He made me feel safe, secure. I wasn't afraid to have my hands on him. I looked at him, naked, and the sight of him didn't make me sick to my stomach. He felt good. Smelled good. Tasted good on my lips and tongue. It was wildly erotic to make him come like that, his cock pulsing between our bodies while he groaned.

I could do that with him again and again. Maybe let him touch *me* a little. With his hands. His mouth. I think I could do it.

But I want more.

I want to be strong enough to let him in. To feel him inside my body. I'm just not sure if I can.

And as for an orgasm? I haven't had one since before Adam.

I've tried. I have what's becoming a collection of vibrators and toys, hoping to find one that will work for me. When I'm by myself, I know I'm safe. I know I'm in control and no one can hurt me. But I still can't do it. I can't climax.

I miss it.

But more than that, I miss being physically intimate with someone without fear. I'm so close to that with Gabriel. Right now, we're in an isolated cabin. I'm in a place that's unfamiliar, and I don't know how long it would take for help to arrive if I needed it. My phone is... I'm not even sure where. And yet, I'm completely relaxed. I'm not afraid.

Gabriel's arm rests against mine. I lean my head against his shoulder and breathe out a long breath. Perhaps this is enough. For now, at least.

He shifts his hand, reaching for mine, and twines our fingers together. He gently rubs his thumb up and down—a leisurely stroke against my finger. Plants a soft kiss on my hair.

I glance up and smile. He looks a little sleepy, his blue eyes half closed. He smiles back and pulls me into his lap, facing him. My arms go around his shoulders, and he wraps his around my back, holding me close. He's safe and warm, his scent masculine and comforting.

He's *safe*.

"It feels so good to be held like this," I say, my voice quiet.

"You feel good," he says.

I turn and press my lips to his neck. His throat vibrates with a soft moan as I work my way up to his ear. He rubs my back and leans his face into me, taking a deep breath into my hair.

"God, I love the way you smell," he says. "It's addictive."

I do the same, breathing him in, my face against his neck. *Addictive* is the word. My brain lights up with endorphins as his scent fills me.

He gently touches my chin and brings my lips to his. The feel of his mouth, his tongue teasing my lips, sends a trail of sparks straight to my core.

He kisses me softly, unhurried, his hands on my back firm, but careful. My body relaxes against him, my arms draped languidly around his neck. His mouth moves against mine, our tongues caressing. He tastes like wine and chocolate.

His hands move slowly up my back and he pulls away slightly. "You don't like it when I do this?" He slides a hand to the back of my neck.

Even though his touch is so soft, I stiffen. "It's my neck." I hesitate; I hate having to relive it. "He—"

Gabriel puts a finger to my lips. "It's okay. You don't have to talk about it if you don't want to. I just want to know what feels good, and what doesn't."

His hand glides down, whispering past my collarbone. "Can I touch you here?" He palms my breast through my shirt.

"Yes," I whisper.

He squeezes gently and I gasp.

"Where else can I touch you?" he asks.

"I don't know."

"Can I try?"

I look into his eyes for a long moment. My body aches for this. My panties are wet and my skin pings with electricity at the thought of him touching me. Touching me *everywhere*.

"Okay."

Please let this work.

We get up and he leads me to the bedroom. His eyes are hungry as he watches me undress. I take off my bra, but keep my panties on. It wouldn't be the first time he's seen me naked, but I can't quite make myself take them off yet.

Gabriel gets undressed, down to his boxer briefs. I lick my lips at the sight of his erection bulging through his underwear.

"Do you want to lie down?" he asks and pulls back the covers.

I nod, and my heart rate speeds up as I lie on the bed.

Gabriel lies down next to me. "Just tell me if you want me to stop."

He traces down my cheek, from my temple to my jaw. I take slow breaths and watch his face as he touches me. His eyes follow his hand as it trails across my upper chest. Moves down to my breasts. He cups one breast and I feel my nipples harden.

My skin tingles as he caresses down my belly. Traces a circle around my belly button, his fingers traveling south. He reaches my panties and touches them gently, his eyes meeting mine. He raises his eyebrows. I nod. *Go ahead.*

He slips his hand beneath the fabric and pauses. Leans in and kisses my forehead, giving me time to decide if I'm okay. His lips brush against mine and he moves his hand lower, lets his fingers whisper across the sensitive skin between my legs. I tip my knees open and let my eyes close.

Gentle fingers stroke me, soft at first. He kisses my jaw and cheek while he explores me. Almost involuntarily, my legs open wider. My breath quickens. Light pressure on my clit makes me gasp and he pulls away.

"Are you okay?" he whispers.

"Yes." I don't even open my eyes. "Please do that again."

He slides his hand down, his movements becoming stronger, more purposeful. Fingers dip inside just enough to glide my wetness across my skin. He finds my clit again and rubs in a gentle rhythm.

Oh my god, it feels so good. Nothing I've ever done myself felt like this. The movement and pressure of his fingers is perfect—slow, rhythmic. I move my hips, grinding against his hand, seeking more. He shifts, moving so he can slide two fingers inside me.

"Oh god, Gabriel."

He pumps his hand faster, pressing against my clit, sliding his fingers in and out. I rock my hips and move my hand down to cover his, guiding him. The heat in my pussy builds until I'm throbbing, desperate for release. He kisses down my chest and his mouth clamps down around my nipple. He sucks, his mouth moving in the same rhythm as his hand. My back arches and I'm aching, pulsing, vibrating with pleasure.

I'm so close, I can barely think. White-hot sparks race through my veins, singeing me from the inside. My core tightens, contracts.

Gabriel drags his jaw up to my neck and growls in my ear. "Come for me, baby."

His voice, his scent, and his fingers working their magic all combine. My pussy clenches and I feel the peak, the summit, the moment before the orgasm erupts.

"Oh Gabriel, please." My voice is breathy, almost strangled. "I'm almost there."

A subtle shift of his hand has me right on the edge. The pressure is almost unbearable, my body frantic.

His mouth next to my ear, his breath hot against my skin, his voice is gravelly and low. "I love you, Sadie."

I come undone.

I burst apart as hot, sweet pulses of ecstasy roll through me, wave after wave. It feels so incredible I can't think, I can't breathe. I clutch his arm, arch my back, roll my hips, call his name.

My breath comes in gasps and I'm covered in a sheen of sweat. Gabriel rests his forehead against mine, his hand still in my panties, his touch suddenly gentle once again.

I let my eyes flutter open and he looks down at me.

"What did you say?" I whisper.

He kisses my nose. "I said I love you." Another kiss to my

forehead. "It's okay. You don't have to say it if you're not ready."

"I love you too. Oh my god, Gabriel, I love you so much."

He wraps his arms around me and holds me close. I cling to him, my heart racing. My body still thrums with heat and pleasure.

"Did that feel good?" he asks quietly.

"That felt amazing," I say.

"Good." He squeezes me tighter. "I can't tell you how much I wanted to do that for you."

"Gabriel, I want you inside me."

"Baby, it's okay. You don't have to."

"I want to." I pull away so I can look him in the eyes. "Please. I want it so badly."

Even with the blissful release of orgasm, my body is begging for more. I want this part of my life back. I want it with Gabriel, and I want it *now*.

"If you're sure," he says.

"I'm positive." My certainty grows with every second that ticks by. "Now. Please."

We both pull off our underwear and I open my legs as he climbs on top of me. I roll my hips and clutch his back, frantic to have him inside me.

The tip of his cock spreads me open and he pushes in, then waits.

"Yes?" he whispers in my ear.

"Yes."

He slides in deeper, a low growl coming from his throat. He takes his time and his cock stretches me, fills me. I've never felt anything like it.

"Tell me if you need me to stop," he says.

"I will," I say, almost breathless. "But don't stop."

His body moves, his cock plunging in and out. I can feel

the strain in his shoulders and arms, how much he's holding back. He's being so careful. And he feels *so good*.

So fucking good.

He kisses above my eyes, my temples, my cheeks. Each corner of my mouth. His cock slides in, like I was made for him. Like we were always meant to be here, tonight. There's no fear. No pain. Nothing but the exquisite pressure of him filling me.

"Are you okay?" he asks, his voice low in my ear.

"Yes."

"I want to fuck you harder."

"Yes," I say. "Harder."

His hips drive into me, burying his cock deep inside. I lean my head back and close my eyes, reveling in the feel of him. His lean body ripples above me, his muscles straining. He groans into my ear, his breath hot against my neck.

"God, Sadie, you feel so good," he says.

"Don't stop," I say, almost breathless. "Don't stop that."

"I could fuck you all night, but I want to come inside you," he says.

My core tightens, the pressure building to a breaking point. Oh my god, I think I might come again. His strong body, braced above me, his skin against mine, his cock sliding in and out of me. It's all so much. So good. So perfect.

I want to feel him unleash.

"Yes, baby," I say. I move my hips, grinding against him. Every movement is agonizing bliss. "Come in me. Do it."

"Fuck, Sadie," he growls. One hand grabs my ass and he pounds me harder. "I love you so much."

His cock thickens, pulsing. I feel my body peaking again, my pussy clenching around him. A few more thrusts and his back stiffens, his body going rigid. He groans, his cock throbs, his come spills into me.

It's all too much.

I explode in a flurry of sparks. My body comes apart beneath him, the tension so sweet. So hot. Pleasure floods through me, radiating from my core. I clutch his back, clinging to him for dear life as the orgasm sweeps me away.

Breathing hard, he kisses me again—soft, gentle kisses on my mouth, my cheeks, my eyelids.

"Are you okay?" he asks.

"Yes," I say. "Oh my god, Gabriel, that was so good. You felt so good."

A broad smile crosses his face. "So much for no orgasms."

I laugh. "You're magic, do you know that?"

He kisses my forehead again. "No, I just love you."

He pulls out and I clean up in the bathroom. When I come out, he's in bed, the sheets pulled up to his waist, showing off his toned body.

I slip in bed next to him and he pulls me close, kissing the top of my head.

"How you doing?" he asks.

"So good," I say. My body feels warm and satisfied. "But Gabriel?"

"Yeah, baby?"

"I should have mentioned this before, but I'm not using anything," I say. "I honestly didn't think I could have sex again after what happened. But you felt so good and I wanted you inside me so badly."

He squeezes me tighter. "It's okay. I didn't stop us either. And honestly, I didn't even bring condoms with me. This was a pretty big surprise. I didn't think you'd be ready."

I look up at him. "You're not upset?"

"Nah," he says. "It was only once. I'll pick up some condoms for next time. You don't need to worry about it."

I stroke my fingers through his chest hair. "You want there to be a next time?"

He rolls me onto my back and holds himself up over me. "I want there to be many next times. But only if that's what you want."

I smile up at him. This wonderful man. So generous and perfect. "Yes, I definitely want that."

He kisses my nose. "Good."

18

SADIE

*M*y fridge is pretty much empty. With a sigh, I close it again. I have a few hours before work, and I should really get some groceries. I can't eat at work—or Gabriel's house—all the time.

Our little getaway was surprising in so many ways. He made me feel amazing. Since then, I've grown more and more comfortable with letting him take the lead. I love how he seems to know my body so well, like he has the power to make it do whatever he wants. And I love giving over that trust to him.

He gave me back something I thought I'd lost.

The last few weeks have been like a dream. He's often busy working, but he always makes time for me, even if it's just a quick lunch date. And if a day goes by and we haven't had a chance to see each other, he coaxes me into staying with him at his place. I love sleeping next to him, my body tucked against his.

I've never really been in love before. Not like this. The way I feel about him crowds out everything else. I'm not preoccupied with difficult memories, nor am I plagued with so many bad dreams. It's like Gabriel fills up all the space in my soul, leaving no room for the pain of the past.

I head to the store to pick up a few things. While I'm walking down the aisle, pushing a small cart, I get a text. I fish my phone out of my purse to check.

Gabriel: Hi lovely. I miss you.

Me: I miss you too. I'll see you at work soon.

Gabriel: I know. Plan on staying with me tonight, okay?

Me: Sounds wonderful.

Gabriel: Love you baby. See you soon.

Me: Love you too.

I let out a contented sigh as I put my phone back in my purse. It probably makes me look silly—like some dreamy little girl—but I don't care. I put back the carton of milk I was going to buy. I doubt I'll be home enough to use it before it expires.

After checking out, I head back to my car. I stuck to mostly non-perishables so I don't have to worry about food going bad. I load the bags into my trunk and walk the cart back to the curb.

When I turn, something catches my eye—movement off to the side of the building. I glance over in time to see someone disappear around the corner of the store. It's a freestanding building with a large parking lot in front, but I don't have a view of that side from where I'm standing.

My stomach turns over and I get the all-too-familiar tingly feeling in my limbs. It has to be a coincidence. No one was watching me. It was just someone walking by.

I take a deep breath, then another, and walk back to my car, telling myself there's nothing to fear.

By the time I'm seated, with my seat belt fastened, my breathing is back to normal. It's been a while since I was hit with such a rush of adrenaline. My hands feel a little shaky, but I pull out of my parking spot, determined to brush off the sensation.

I stop at the entrance to the street and glance in my rear-view mirror. There's a man standing next to a silver car, watching me. My heart nearly stops and it feels like the air is sucked out of my lungs. It looks like Adam.

I squeeze my eyes shut. *It can't be. Please, it can't be him.*

But when I look again, he's gone.

Did I imagine it? Was it just some random shopper who happened to be looking in my direction?

The sick feeling in my stomach spreads. I leave the parking lot, but I don't go straight home. I wind around the streets for a while, checking my rear-view mirror constantly to make sure I'm not being followed.

Maybe I'm being paranoid. Maybe it wasn't him. But I'm not going to take any chances.

I GET into work a little early. I haven't quite shaken off the feeling that someone was watching me at the store, and I feel safer here. A quick check of the reservations shows we're booked up; it's going to be a busy night.

"Hey, Sadie."

I turn around to find Linda, the business manager.

"Something came in the mail for you," she says, holding out an envelope.

I hesitate before taking it out of her hand. My heart leaps and I struggle to keep my expression neutral. "Um, that's strange. I don't know why I'd be getting mail here."

"It is strange," she says, her forehead crinkling. "But it's addressed to you, so..."

I glance at the outside. It is addressed to me, care of the Ocean Mark Restaurant, at this address. There's no return address and the postmark is Ogden, Utah.

"Thanks," I say, amazed that my voice sounds so steady. Linda smiles and heads back to her office.

Utah? Adam doesn't live in Utah, so maybe this isn't from him. Granted, I don't know anyone in Utah. I briefly stopped there on my way west, but I didn't stay long. And I certainly didn't meet anyone who would send me something in the mail.

My hands tremble and my heart races as I slide my finger beneath the flap, breaking the seal. There's a folded piece of paper inside. I take it out and open it.

My stomach rolls over and bile burns the back of my throat. I stare at it, my eyes wide. It's a printout of the photos from the *Simple Pleasures* article. In both of them, I'm circled with a red pen. At the top is a single word.

Mine.

I look on the back, but it's blank. There's nothing else. No name. No return address on the envelope. Just this photo and that one word.

Oh my god.

Gabriel isn't in his office. I find him in the dining room, talking with Sam.

"Can I talk to you for a minute?" I ask.

"Of course."

He gives a few last instructions to Sam and leads me to his office, his hand gentle on the small of my back. When we get inside, he closes the door behind us.

"Is everything okay?"

I'm trying so hard to hold it together, but my hand shakes when I hold up the printout. "No. This came in the mail for me."

Gabriel takes it out of my hand. His face clouds over with anger. "Did this come to your house? Or here?"

"Here." I hand him the envelope.

"Utah?" he asks.

"I don't know," I say. "Adam lives in Missouri. Or he did, at least. I guess he could have had it sent from Utah so I wouldn't know it was him? Maybe he knows someone there?"

He pulls out his phone and taps on the screen a few times.

"What are you looking for?" I ask.

"What's the name of your hometown?"

"Jackson City."

He taps a few more times, then holds up his phone. It's a map.

"If you were going to drive from Jackson City, Missouri to here, it would take you through Ogden, Utah."

I clap my hand over my mouth.

"Hey," he says, his voice soothing. He puts the paper down on his desk and runs his hands up and down my arms. "He's not going to hurt you. I won't let anything happen to you."

I take a trembling breath. "He's here, Gabriel. He knows where I am and he's here. I think I saw him."

"Where?"

"When I was at the grocery store earlier," I say, clutching my stomach. I think I might vomit. "I thought I saw someone watching me, but when I looked again, he was gone. But I think it was him. He knows I work here."

"Sadie," Gabriel says, his voice firm. He grabs me by the upper arms and holds me steady. "Listen. I'm not going to let anything happen to you. I don't care if he's in town. He can't hurt you. Baby, I swear, I won't let him touch you."

I step into him and he wraps his arms around me, kissing the top of my head. "You don't understand. He'll never stop. I don't know what he'll do."

"If he shows up, we'll deal with him." He rubs slow circles across my back. "But I don't want you to be alone. You should come stay with me. Not just for tonight."

"Are you sure?"

"Absolutely. I want you with me. Plus, my house has a home security system. We'll go to your place after work and get what you need."

Relief floods through me and I nod against his chest. The idea of being in my house alone, knowing Adam is out there, is terrifying.

Gabriel pulls back and touches my face. "You'll stay with me until..." He hesitates, his eyes searching mine. "I guess until we're sure you're safe."

"Thank you."

He leans for a kiss. "Don't worry."

"What if he comes here?"

His eyes narrow and his shoulders tighten. "I *hope* he comes here. Then I can deal with him."

"Oh god, Gabriel, don't kill him," I say.

"You don't want him gone?"

I step back. "I do, but what if you went to prison? You can't."

He laughs, but there's little humor in it. "Don't worry, baby, I'm not going to murder anyone. But if he comes anywhere near you, I'll make sure he never does it again."

19

GABE

*S*adie unpacks a few things into drawers I hastily cleared for her. I don't want her to feel like she has to live out of a bag while she's here, and I certainly have enough space. We made a quick stop at her house on the way home from the restaurant so she could grab some of her things. I did a circuit through the house while she waited near the front door. I wanted to make sure everything was okay before I let her go inside.

It's late, so we both change for bed. She stands next to me at the double vanity in my bathroom while we brush our teeth and it feels... right. Like she belongs here.

Maybe it's too soon to ask her to move in with me officially, but I'm tempted. It's more than my concerns for her safety. I want her here because I'm in love with her. The more I think about it, the more sure I become. I want to share my life with her.

But tonight isn't the time for big decisions. We're both tired, and I know everything that happened today made her edgy. To her credit, she handled the dinner service perfectly. I almost asked her if she wanted to go home, but to be honest, I wanted her there, where I could protect her. She didn't let fear get the better of her, and even now, I can see the strength in her eyes.

I don't think she gives herself enough credit for how strong she is. She's amazing.

We slip between the sheets. I prefer to sleep naked, and Sadie doesn't mind. She snuggles up against me, her back to my front. I love that she doesn't hesitate to let me touch her. I slide my hand beneath her tank top and cup her breast. Her nipple hardens against my palm and I kiss her shoulder.

"Mm," she says. "If you keep doing that, you better mean it."

I flick my tongue over the dusting of freckles on her shoulder and press my erection into her ass. "I mean it."

She arches her back and I slip her panties down so I can press my cock against her bare skin. She rubs against me while I kiss her neck. I reach around, sliding my hand down her belly to the soft skin between her legs. She's already wet and she presses her ass against me harder when I start rubbing her clit.

"You make me feel so good," she whispers.

"I love making you feel good."

As much as I'm enjoying the feel of her ass grinding into me, I move away and gently nudge her onto her back. She raises her arms so I can take off her shirt, and I toss it to the side. I kiss down her neck to her breasts, sucking on each nipple while I keep stimulating her clit. She moans as I work my way down, caressing her soft skin with my lips.

When I reach her center, I position myself between her legs. She stiffens a little so I rub my jaw against her inner thighs and plant soft kisses outside her pussy. Her breathing quickens and her legs relax.

I slide my tongue up her center, tasting her, and groan with pleasure. "God Sadie, you taste so good."

Before she can answer, I go to work on her clit, exploring her. I feel for her body's responses as I lick and suck. She gasps and moans, clutching the sheets.

"Oh, Gabriel... How are you... That's so... Don't stop."

I push her legs back and increase the pace, using my tongue in a steady rhythm. She goes wild, losing control, and I feel her orgasm peak. I don't let up, bringing her to climax again, making one orgasm roll right into the next. When she finally comes down, gasping for breath, I kiss her gently, working my way back up her body.

"How did you do that?" she says, still panting.

I reach for a condom and quickly slip it on, then climb on top of her. She lifts her head to bring her lips to mine and I kiss her deeply, letting her taste pass between us.

"Baby, every bit of you tastes so good," I say. "I could do that to you forever."

Instead of holding myself braced above her, I lower down and rest my forearms beneath her shoulders. It puts more of our skin in contact. I grab her shoulders from behind and hold her while I slip my cock inside. She's so wet, I slide in easily, her heat enveloping me.

My hips move and this angle presses my pelvis against her clit with every thrust. She already came for me—at least twice—but I want to make her come again. I love being the one to make her let loose—love feeling her succumb to my body. I know it's not something she gives easily, and I cherish it.

Plus, she feels fucking amazing.

I kiss her neck while I fuck her, sucking on her soft skin, tasting her sweetness. She clutches my back, her legs wrapped around me, her pussy blissfully tight. I can feel her heat build and it urges me on. I thrust harder, faster, holding her with my hands beneath shoulders. Her hard nipples press against my chest, every bit of skin that touches hers lighting up with electricity.

I'm consumed by her. The feel of her body and her scent on my sheets. Her taste on my tongue. The pressure builds almost to a breaking point, our bodies moving together as one. I groan against her neck and she pants my name with every breath.

Her body spasms beneath me, her pussy suddenly clenching around my cock. Fuck, she feels so good when she comes. My eyes roll back, my body goes rigid, and I unleash inside her. My cock pulses hard, the sensation overwhelming. I drive into her while she digs her fingers into my back.

My breath comes fast, my chest pressed against hers. She holds me tight for long moments, and I wait, enjoying the feel of her body beneath me. Eventually I get up and deal with the condom, then crawl back in bed with her. She smiles at me, her eyes dreamy and sated. I pull her into my arms, take a deep breath of her scent, and settle in to sleep.

SOMETHING JOLTS ME AWAKE. It takes me a second to realize my phone is ringing. I grab it and look at the time; it's just after three. A hit of adrenaline surges through me and I sit up. Something must be wrong.

"Hello?"

Sadie rolls over and blinks.

"Mr. Parker?" I don't recognize the man's voice on the other end.

"Yes, is something wrong?"

"This is Stewart Watson with the Jetty Beach Fire

Department," he says. "Are you the owner of the Ocean Mark?"

"Yes."

"Mr. Parker, there's a fire at your restaurant," he says. "We got the call about fifteen minutes ago. Someone drove by and saw the flames. A unit has already responded and they're working to control the blaze."

I'm up and out of bed before I realize what I'm doing. "I'll be right there." I hang up and toss the phone on my bed.

"What's wrong?" Sadie asks.

"There's a fire at the restaurant."

"Oh my god."

I jam my legs into a pair of jeans. "You don't have to get up."

"Of course I'm coming with you." She's already half dressed.

My mind is spinning on the drive up the coast. It's the longest twenty minutes of my life. I grip the steering wheel, my knuckles white from the strain. Sadie is silent in the passenger seat, her face turned toward the window, her hands clutched together in her lap.

I see the glow before the restaurant comes into view. Flickering orange light dances on the surrounding trees and reflects off the clouds. In the darkness I can just make out a black cloud of smoke billowing into the night sky.

I whip around the hard left to the restaurant. Two fire trucks are parked in front, their lights flashing in the night. I park at the edge of the lot and throw open my door. The heat beats at me, even from this distance.

Everything seems to be moving in slow motion. The fire-fighters with their hoses. The fire chief shouting instructions. Flames shooting out the roof. I hear glass shattering, the dull roar of the fire. The whine of a siren as another fire truck arrives. The air smells of choking smoke.

There's nothing I can do.

I stand next to the car, staring at my restaurant. It's engulfed in flames, much of one side already crumbling, the wood beams turning to ash and glowing cinders. Despite the yelling, the men running, the reinforcements arriving, I know it's already over. They won't be able to save it. The best they can do is contain it and keep it from spreading.

I put a hand on my car to steady myself. This place is my life. I put everything I have into my restaurant. All my money. My time. My energy. Everything. This place was my dream.

Now all I can do is stand here and watch it burn.

A wave of emptiness washes over me. I'm numb, as if my ability to feel is being burned away to ash. I can't feel the heat of the fire. The acrid tang of smoke is gone. Even in my darkest moments, I've never felt this hollow. Gutted.

Helpless.

I'm startled by the feel of someone next to me. Sadie slips her hand into mine and squeezes. I glance at her face; she's horror-stricken as she watches the restaurant burn.

A fireman walks over to talk to me. I drop Sadie's hand and step forward, bracing myself for what I already know he's going to say.

There's nothing more they can do.

20

SADIE

*M*y eyes are heavy, but I can't sleep. I'm lying on Gabriel's couch, curled up with a navy throw blanket. Despite my exhaustion, I keep staring at the ceiling. I'm too worried to rest.

We were at the restaurant until after dawn, watching it burn, waiting for news. It was one of the most horrifying experiences of my life—and that's saying something. The blaze was huge by the time we got there, and no matter how hard the fire fighters worked, it ripped through the building as if it were nothing but dry grass.

By the time the sun rose, the worst of it was out, but the extent of the damage was clear. The entire building was ruined.

Gabriel spoke with the fire chief for a long time while I sat in the car and waited. Eventually, he came back and drove us to his place. He said they told him to go home and they'd call him with news. They still needed to investigate to determine the cause of the fire.

I thought we'd go back to bed and at least try to get some sleep, but Gabriel dropped me off. He said he was too restless to wait at home. After making sure I'd be okay, and double checking the security system, as well as the locks on all the doors and windows, he left, telling me he'd text me with news.

I turn over, pulling the blanket over my shoulder. I'm so worried about Gabriel. He didn't seem upset. Quite the opposite, in fact. He was calm, unemotional. I think it would have been easier if he'd shown some of what he was feeling. His stoic face was unnerving. Almost scary.

My phone *bings* and I snatch it off the coffee table.

Gabriel: They think it was arson. I'll be home in a little while.

I stare at the screen, at those words, and a sick feeling spreads through my stomach. Arson. Someone started that fire. Someone did this to him intentionally.

I put a hand to my mouth, bile burning the back of my throat. I know, without a shadow of a doubt, who did this. It was Adam.

The flowers. The printout of my photo. I know I saw him in town. He's been here, waiting—watching. I was afraid he'd attack me. That he'd corner me in a parking lot or come to Gabriel's house when I was alone. But he didn't.

He did something worse.

I get up and pace around the room. It's only a matter of time before he finds me. If he's capable of something like this, there's no telling what else he might do. Does he know that Gabriel and I are together? Did he do this in a fit of jealous rage?

Whatever his reasoning, this is a clear message. He's willing to go to great lengths to hurt me. And to hurt the people I love.

My heart beats faster and I look out the front window

every time I pass. Is he out there? Does he know where I am?

Will he burn down Gabriel's house next?

This is my fault. Gabriel never asked for this. I stood by his side while we watched his restaurant burn to the ground, and it was *my* fault. If I'd never come here—if I'd never met Gabriel—his restaurant would still be standing. I don't know where *I* would be, but at least his dream wouldn't have been taken from him.

It's hard to breathe. I walk back into the bedroom and look around. At my things on the nightstand. My clothes on a chair. My bag tucked away in a corner, as if it won't be needed again. I can see my makeup bag, lotion, and hair products on the bathroom counter. All unpacked, like I live here.

I grab my bag and start shoving things into it. I can't stay. Adam is going to find me. He probably already knows where I am. He could be outside, watching Gabriel's house, hiding in the ditch across the street. If I don't get out of town—fast—he's going to get to me. If he's willing to commit arson, what else will he do?

I know the answer to that. He'll do anything.

He brutally raped me, as if the act of violating my body would make me belong to him. When that didn't work, he started following me again. Stalking me. It was only a matter of time before he did something else. Before he raped me again.

Or worse.

The fact that I disappeared seems to have pushed him further over the edge. He's dangerous, and if I know anything about him, he'll have done everything he can to hide what he did. The authorities won't be able to pin the fire on him. It won't matter what I say; I'll tell them what I know, but it won't be enough. We won't have proof, and he'll walk. He'll be free to keep terrorizing me.

I only have one choice. I have to run.

I finish packing my things and wait by the front door. My car is just outside. Can I make it? Will he be there when I go outside? I wish I knew. I peek through the curtains a dozen times before I gather the courage to open the door, my bag slung over my shoulder, pepper spray in one hand, keys in the other. I rush out to my car and throw my things inside, locking the doors as soon as I'm in. A quick glance around shows the coast seems to be clear, but I'm not taking any chances.

I take a round-about route out of town, winding through back roads before I finally get to the highway. My eyes dart to my rearview mirror constantly, looking for any sign of someone following me. I don't see anyone behind; the road is mostly clear.

My hands grip the steering wheel and I take shaking breaths. I have to get away. I have to leave before he can find me. Before he can find Gabriel.

I'm strangely calm as the distance between me and Jetty Beach grows, and I consider my options. Where should I go? A small town was a mistake. I thought going to a place no one in Missouri had ever heard of would make it easier to stay hidden. But in a small town, there are too many ways to be seen. Too many people who know you.

A big city would be a better choice. You can get lost as one of millions. I want to stay on one of the coasts; middle America will always feel like a trap to me. I could cross the country and head for New York. It seems like it would be easy to get lost there. Blend in. But Los Angeles is closer. Less chance of my car breaking down. If I can make it to L.A., I can sell my car. Maybe live without one for a while.

I'll live under an assumed name until I can change it legally. My name won't appear anywhere.

I'll dye my hair, do whatever it takes to stay hidden. No more restaurant jobs. No more friends. No more connections.

It's the only way.

Nausea roils through me again. Gabriel. Leaving him like this is devastating. But if I wait to tell him goodbye, I know my resolve will crumble. I'll let him talk me into staying. And I won't be safe, and neither will he. He already lost his restaurant because of me. I can't put him in that position. I love him too much to do that to him.

Tears roll down my cheeks. I'm so sick of crying. Sick of living in fear.

I'm sure the fire at Gabriel's restaurant will make the local news. I already know I'm going to send the article to my family. They won't believe it's Adam. They'll write back and tell me I'm paranoid. That I'm trying to hurt him again. But I don't care. I know the truth. I know he did this. I'll tell them what happened and let them know that's the last time they'll hear from me.

And I won't speak to them ever again.

I'm utterly alone in the world, but that's how it has to be. I don't have any other choice. Not if I want to get away from Adam.

Not if I want to make sure he doesn't hurt anyone else I love.

21

GABE

*T*he smell of wet ash permeates the air. I step carefully through the charred remains of the Ocean Mark. I have no idea what I'm looking for. Nothing is salvageable. The entire building, and everything in it, is ruined. But despite my exhaustion, I can't stop picking through the rubble.

Two fire fighters and several police officers are still here. They found the source of the fire and there's evidence of an accelerant. Whoever did this clearly intended to make sure it burned to the ground.

They asked me dozens of questions, establishing where I was last night. Who has access to the building. Do I have any enemies? Disgruntled former employees? Someone with a grudge?

I told the police about Adam Cooper and his history with Sadie. I was glad they took my information seriously. It's a tenuous connection, especially considering we can only speculate that he's in the area. But I believe Sadie saw him, and the printout of her photos proves he knows she worked here. He's here, and I'm sure he did this.

A car pulls up and Finn and Lucas get out. They both stare, wide eyed, at the remains of the restaurant. I texted them both, so they knew what to expect, but I guess seeing it in person is still a shock.

"Oh fuck, Gabe," Finn says as he walks toward me. "You said fire, but... holy shit."

I step over a blackened wood beam, brushing my hands together. "Yeah, it's bad."

"That's the understatement of the century," Lucas says. "Do you know what happened?"

"They think arson," I say.

"You're fucking with me," Lucas says.

"No," I say. "Someone started it."

"Holy shit... again," Finn says.

"God, I'm such an asshole," Lucas says. "The first thing that crosses my mind is a joke about you wanting the insurance money, but this just isn't funny."

Finn glares at Lucas.

"What?" Lucas asks.

"Insurance money? Seriously?" Finn says.

"I said it was an asshole thing to think," Lucas says. "And I didn't tell the joke."

I laugh and shake my head. It's kind of amazing that in the midst of the ruins of my life's work, my best friends can still make me laugh.

"Was anyone here?" Finn asks. "No one got hurt, did they?"

"No," I say. "It was late. Well after everyone went home."

"Do you have any idea who did it?" Lucas asks, his voice quiet.

"Yeah. Possibly."

They both look at me with raised eyebrows.

"Sadie has someone after her," I say. "She left Missouri to get away from him, but he found out where she is—at least where she works. He sent her some things and she saw him in town. Then, this happened."

"Holy fuck," Lucas says.

"I know. Believe me, I know. It's fucking crazy."

"Where's Sadie now?" Finn asks.

"She stayed at my place," I say. "I didn't want her to be alone if this guy was around."

"Good," Finn says.

Another car pulls up and Clover jumps out of the passenger seat. She stops dead in her tracks, her hands over her mouth, her eyes huge. Cody gets out and walks around the car to stand behind her.

"Oh no," she says, her voice breaking. "No, no, no."

"It'll be okay," I say, trying to sound sure of myself. Although I feel anything but.

She puts her arms around me and squeezes me tight. I hug her back. She loved this place too. It was home to her in much the same way it was for me.

I realize, looking at the blackened wood, that I'm at a crossroads.

I set my sights on the Ocean Mark before I had any formal training as a chef. This was the place where it all began—my love of food, of cooking. It was always my dream to settle here and run this restaurant. Live in my hometown. I gave up a lot for this place. I could have had a much different career—a much different life. I could be living in a big city, cooking somewhere trendy. Somewhere progressive. That was what Amanda wanted. She thought this wasn't good enough for me. It wasn't big enough. It certainly wasn't enough for her.

Now I have to decide what I want. What's enough for *me*.

It's amazing what happens when everything is stripped away. So much becomes clear. I just lost everything, and yet I didn't. I have everything I could ever want.

I have Sadie.

I don't know what's going to happen to this place. Will I be able to rebuild? Will I even want to? Right now, I can't say.

But with Sadie in my life, this building doesn't matter. Not like it once did. I have some big decisions to make, but one thing is certain. I want a life with Sadie. Protecting her. Taking care of her. Loving her.

I want that with a fierceness that takes my breath away.

I do my best to comfort Clover, although Cody still has to lead her back to their car with tears running down her cheeks. I say thank you and goodbye to Finn and Lucas, assuring them I'll be fine. It's a fucked up situation, but I have a handle on it.

And I need to get back to my girl.

When I pull up to my house, my exhaustion vanishes at the sight of the empty driveway. Where is she? I don't like the thought of her leaving without me. Adam could come after her, especially if he finds her alone.

I fire off a text to her before I get out of the car, asking where she is. She probably needed something from the store. That's my fault for leaving her alone so long. I didn't want to make her stay at the restaurant. She needed some sleep, so I left her here so she could rest. But I was gone a lot longer than anticipated.

Inside, I find a throw blanket draped over the couch. I check my phone again, realizing she never texted me back after I let her know the fire chief determined it was arson. Did she get my text? I would have thought she'd have answered me. I know we're both thinking the same thing—we know who did this. I was going to tell her more details, but figured it would be better to discuss it in person. We could talk about what happened, and how to move forward. Start discussing the future.

It's odd that she didn't answer.

I grab a piece of bread leftover from dinner last night. The silence sits heavily over the house, thick like a dense fog.

Where is she?

I check the bedroom and something seems off. It looks too empty. I glance into the bathroom, at the bare counter. Did she put her things somewhere else before? Or were they still sitting out? I can't remember for sure.

A sense of dread steals over me. I check the closet, the drawers she was using. Nothing. Her things aren't there.

Oh fuck. She's gone.

IT'S HARD NOT to panic. I drive around town, looking for her car, but I don't see any sign of her. Deep down, I know she left town. Why, I can't understand. Doesn't she trust me to take care of her? To protect her?

Another thought rattles its way around my brain. What if he got to her?

But she wouldn't have driven away, would she? Not in her car. If Adam took her, they wouldn't have taken the time to pack her things. It's not like she would have gone willingly.

I'm going to need help if I'm going to track her down. I stop and send a text to Hunter. If anyone has the resources to find her, it's him. I don't wait for a reply, just head straight for his house.

Hunter opens the door shortly after I knock.

"Hey man," he says, his voice hushed. "I just put Sebastian down for a nap. Come on in."

I follow him inside, stepping over a little pile of green army men in the hall.

"Emma took Isaac to get some new shoes," Hunter says. "They'll be back in a little while. What's up?"

"Sadie's gone," I say. I don't have time for small talk. "I think she left town."

"What?" he asks. "What happened?"

I tell him everything, keeping certain details vague to protect Sadie's privacy. I can tell by the way his expression darkens that he understands.

"So I think the most likely suspect in the fire is him," I say. "I'm sure she's thinking it too. But I didn't have a chance to talk to her about it. I got home just a little while ago and she was gone. I checked her house, and she's not there either. I drove around town a little, to see if I could find her car. Maybe I'm being crazy, but she's not answering her phone and her stuff is gone."

"Do you think he took her?"

"Her car is gone," I say. "And she packed her things."

"Not consistent with a kidnapping, no. Okay, so we have a search and retrieval," Hunter says, suddenly all business. He goes into the kitchen and pulls a small spiral notebook and pen out of a drawer, then flips it open and starts writing. "Locate Sadie, bring her back safely. Shouldn't be an issue, since I know her license plate number. I know a guy. He should be able to pinpoint her location pretty quickly."

"Wait, why do you know Sadie's license plate number?" I ask.

He gives me a sheepish look and shrugs his shoulders. "I remember things like that. I kind of can't help it."

"Well, I'm glad," I say. "You know a guy?"

"Yeah, don't ask too many questions," he says. "Second, we need to find this Adam douchecanoe. You're sure he's in town?"

"He's been in the area," I say. "Sadie saw him, but only once."

"What else can you give me?"

I rub my jaw. "He's from Missouri. Sadie said he used to drive a black Ford pickup, but she can't be sure he still does." I pull out my phone and find him on Facebook; Sadie showed it to me once. Most of his profile is private—there's not much I can see. But his profile picture is clear. "That's him."

Hunter clears his throat and when he speaks, his voice is quiet and serious. "Gabe, do you want me to have him taken care of?"

I pause, not quite sure if he means what I think he means. "What, like...?"

He holds eye contact and raises his eyebrows, just slightly.

Does it make me a terrible person that I'm considering this?

I run a hand through my hair and blow out a breath. I want him out of Sadie's life, and god knows the guy doesn't deserve to keep wasting oxygen. But murder? I don't think I can go that far. And I really don't want to put my brother-in-law in that position.

"I don't think that's the answer," I say. "And I can't ask you to do something like that."

He nods, his face solemn. "Let me know if you change your mind. In the meantime, we need to get eyes on him. I wish you would have told me sooner. I could have done something before he fucking torched your restaurant."

"I had no idea he'd do something like that," I say. "And I know he's still a problem, but right now, I just want to find Sadie."

"Don't worry, man," he says. "We'll find her."

22

SADIE

*A*lthough I'd rather not use my debit card at all, I left town with only about twenty dollars in my wallet, so I don't have much choice. I hand it to the clerk at the front desk and glance over my shoulder. I suppose I should stop doing that. I've been driving for hours, and there's no sign that Adam followed me. Still, the prickly feeling on the back of my neck won't go away, and I keep expecting to turn and see him standing there.

The motel is cheap, but as long as it's clean, I'll deal. I just need to get some sleep before I keep going.

"How many nights?" the clerk asks.

"Just one."

She nods, her expression bored.

I get my room key. It's a two-story building, with doors that open to the outside. A place with interior entrances would have been better. Somehow that feels safer. But I'm in the middle of nowhere, and this run-down motel is the best I'm going to get unless I want to keep driving. Which I don't. So I head upstairs to room two-ten and unlock the door.

It's typical—garish turquoise and salmon comforter, blue carpet, a cheap painting on the wall that looks vaguely like a sunset. It smells like lemon cleanser and bleach, and it looks clean. I toss my bag on the bed and check the bathroom. The sink is cracked, but the towels are fresh. It will do.

I pull out my phone. Gabriel keeps trying to call. I feel horrible for ignoring him. I know he's worried. It was a huge mistake to get involved with him in the first place. I was so stupid for underestimating the risk. What else did I think Adam would do if he found out I was with someone? The more I think about it, the more convinced I become that getting to Gabriel is why he started the fire. Just the fact that I work there isn't motive enough.

He wanted to send a clear message that he won't let someone else have me. That he'll punish anyone who tries.

I can't do that to Gabriel. I can't ask him to live with that danger. Leaving him like this makes me sick to my stomach. I honestly don't know what I'm doing anymore. When he told me it was arson, I panicked. Maybe I should have stayed.

But I can't get rid of the memory of what it felt like to stand with him and watch his restaurant burn. How could I possibly stay after that? I love him too much to put him in that kind of danger.

My only hope is that Adam will realize I'm gone and leave Jetty Beach. I don't know how long I can stay hidden from him. I'll do a better job this time. I won't use my name. I won't make friends. Maybe I'll keep moving. Stay in L.A. for a while, and move on before he has a chance to find me. If I stay one step ahead of him, he might never catch up.

I don't know why I do this to myself, but I sit on the edge of the bed and read Gabriel's texts again.

Baby, where are you?

Are you okay?

Baby, what's going on? Where are you?

I'm getting really worried. Please text me back.

Sadie, what happened? Where did you go?

I squeeze my eyes shut. I'll answer him in the morning, just before I get on the highway again. I want to tell him how sorry I am. How much I love him. But maybe making a clean break is better. I should tell him it's over.

My entire body aches at the thought of typing those words. No one ever said life is fair, but this is leaving me desolate.

That fucker Adam keeps taking everything from me. He violated my body, destroyed my trust. He took my family, my hometown. And now this. My Gabriel.

It's so goddamn unfair.

I don't bother getting undressed—just push my bag aside and get beneath the covers. I'm too exhausted to do anything else. I can't even find the energy to cry.

A SHARP PAIN wakes me with a start. Bile burns the back of my throat and my stomach heaves. Oh god, I'm going to—

I run to the bathroom, my hand clamped over my mouth. I barely make it to the toilet before I vomit up what's left of last night's fast-food dinner. A cold sweat breaks out over my forehead, and I wait a few minutes, taking deep breaths, before I get up.

I feel hungover, but I certainly wasn't drinking last night. My stomach is raw and I'm not sure that's the only trip to the bathroom I'll make. I clean up as best I can in the sink and splash some cold water on my face. Glancing in the mirror, I cringe. My skin is pallid, my eyes sunken.

Just what I need, to be sick on the road.

I go back to bed and lie down, hoping my stomach will settle. After a few minutes, it starts to get better, the nausea fading to a mild ache.

The thought of food sounds awful, so I decide not to worry about breakfast. I'll just change my clothes and get going.

Gingerly, I get up, not wanting to trigger another vomiting spell. So far, so good. I put on a clean shirt and go into the bathroom to brush out my hair and put it up in a bun.

Standing in front of the mirror with my hair halfway tied, I stop and stare at my reflection.

Wait.

I don't feel sick anymore. If I had food poisoning, it would last for hours. A virus? It wouldn't disappear after I vomit once. I'd have other symptoms—a fever. Something.

But I actually feel okay.

There's another reason a woman might vomit out of nowhere. Especially in the morning.

Oh my god.

My hands shake and I swallow hard, putting my brush down on the counter. I glance down at my belly. Is it possible? Am I pregnant?

I can't deny that it's *possible*. We had unprotected sex at the cabin. But it was just the one time. What are the chances?

As much as I want to put more distance between myself and Jetty Beach, now that I've had the thought, I can't escape it. I have to know.

There's a convenience store across the street. I try to act calm while the cashier rings up my purchase, but my hands won't stop trembling. I manage to pay and I take it back to my room.

I go into the bathroom, and for the second time in my life, I wait to find out if I'm pregnant.

The first time was after Adam. I took dozens of tests, terrified he'd gotten me pregnant. I took them well before they're supposed to be effective, and didn't stop until I got my period.

Then, I prayed for it to be negative. Now? I have no idea what to think.

What if it's positive? What if I'm having Gabriel's baby?

The storm of emotions inside me is so overwhelming, I'm almost numb. I lean against the door frame, afraid I might fall over.

Obviously, I should hope it's negative. I can't have a baby. I'm on the run, trying to get away from the man who won't stop tormenting me. I can't bring a child into that life.

On the other hand, Gabriel's baby...

No, I can't let myself indulge in fantasies like that. It *has* to be negative.

I go back into the bathroom to check the test. I take a deep breath before I pick it up, and make myself look.

Pregnant.

The test drops from my limp fingers to clatter on the dingy linoleum floor. My heart races and my breath comes fast. Pregnant? I'm pregnant?

Oh my god, Adam is going to kill me.

If he finds me, and discovers I'm having another man's baby, he'll kill me. Literally. He'll kill Gabriel too. I know it, deep in my soul. Burning down the restaurant shows how unstable he is. He's insane. He wants me for himself, like I'm his property. And when he finds out another man has had me, he's going to lose his mind.

What the hell am I going to do now?

23

SADIE

I literally have no idea where I'm going to go.

I'm sitting in my car, still parked in the motel parking lot. The positive pregnancy test is sticking out of my purse, half encased in the wrapper. Maybe I should have thrown it away, but it's like I need to keep looking at it to believe it's real.

My phone sits in my lap. I've almost called Gabriel at least ten times. I can't just leave him when I'm carrying his child. I don't want to leave him at all.

I feel like I'm being torn in half, the pieces of myself raw and bleeding. Gabriel means everything to me. He showed me that I can trust again. That I'm capable of love, and being loved. He gently drew out a piece of me I thought was dead and gone. He was patient, and steadfast. He never once doubted me or my story. He believed me. He believed *in* me.

In *us*.

But Adam won't ever leave me alone. And if he gets the chance, he's going to kill me. If I'm with Gabriel, he'll kill him too.

A car pulls up directly behind mine, blocking my way

out. My heart instantly starts racing and a surge of adrenaline pours through my system. I reach for my purse, my
hands shaking, and fumble for the pepper spray I always
carry.

Oh my god, he found me.

My fight or flight response is going crazy. I shove the
pregnancy test deeper into my purse. I can't let Adam see it.
Maybe I can still talk my way out of this—but not if he
knows I'm pregnant. That's going to send him off the
deep end.

"Sadie."

The voice is slightly muffled from outside my car. He's
standing next to my door, his hand pulling up on the
handle. It's locked.

But the voice isn't Adam's.

I make myself look up through the window. There's a
man there, tall and strong, with dexterous hands, stubble on
his jaw, and unkempt dark blond hair. Piercing blue eyes
look down at me, pleading.

It's Gabriel.

I gasp in a hard breath and press every button on the
door, trying to get it unlocked. Tears of shock and relief blur
my vision. Finally, the door unlocks and he throws it open.
Hands grasp me, pulling me out, crushing me against his
body.

"Oh my god, Sadie."

I melt into him, giving in. I don't have it in me to resist,
and I don't want to. He's here. I don't know how he found
me, but he did.

He holds me tight, his arms wrapped firmly around me.
I thread my arms around his waist and bury my face in his
chest, breathing him in. His masculine scent fills me. Calms
me. I close my eyes and cling to him—to the hope that

surges through me at his presence.

"Baby, what happened?" he asks, his voice soft.

I take a shaky breath. "He's going to kill me."

"No." He pulls back and presses his palm to the side of my face. "Sadie, I swear to you, I won't let that happen. He'll never hurt you. I promise."

"He burned down your restaurant," I say. "That's how insane he is."

"Don't worry about the restaurant," he says. "It's just a building."

"But Gabriel—"

"Shh," he says, putting a finger to my lips. "Is that why you left? Because you're afraid of him?"

I nod. "If he's crazy enough to commit arson, I don't know what else he'll do. He won't stop."

"I'll deal with him," Gabriel says. "We'll figure this out, together. But I can't protect you if you take off like this."

"I was trying to protect *you*."

He leans in and kisses me. "Oh my sweet Sadie. You don't have to protect me."

"Yes, I do. I love you. I can't let him ruin your life the way he ruined mine."

"The only thing that will ruin my life is losing you. And I'll be damned if I let him take you away from me." He kisses me again. "Please come home. I promise I'll keep you safe if you just come home with me."

I gape at him. What did I ever do to deserve such a wonderful man? "Okay. I'll come."

He hugs me again, sighing out a long breath, like he's relieved. I bask in the comfort of his arms, the steadiness of his body against mine, the assurance of his safety. I don't know what this means, or how we're going to make this work. I don't have any idea how to stop Adam. But I know I can't live without Gabriel.

"I'm so sorry I ran," I say into his chest. "I never wanted to leave you. I was just so scared."

"I know, baby," he says, stroking my hair. "I know."

"Gabriel, there's something I need to tell you." Maybe now isn't the best moment, but I can't wait. I can't hold this inside.

He leans back so he can meet my eyes. "Of course. What is it?"

Deep breath. "I'm pregnant."

He blinks and for a second, he's expressionless. "You're...?"

I nod and start talking, the words spilling out in a rush. "I didn't know when I left yesterday. I took a test this morning. I've been sitting here trying to figure out what to do. I'm so sorry. I think it must have happened our first time, when we were at the cabin and—"

He shuts me up with his lips, taking my mouth in a hungry kiss. It's deep and passionate, his tongue caressing mine. For the briefest second, I wonder whether we're alone in this parking lot, but the thought flees almost as fast as it came. I'm consumed by him, swept up in this moment—in the feel of our bodies pressed together, in his devastating kiss.

When he finally pulls away, he cups my face with his hands. "I love you."

"You're not upset?" I ask.

He smiles. The man who just lost everything *smiles* at me. "How could I be? Don't you see? Everything we've both been through brought us here, to this moment. I'd do anything to spare you the pain you've endured. But if things were different, you might never have left Missouri. You'd still be living in that same town, thousands of miles away from me." He pauses to kiss me again. "I can't tell you how often I doubted my decision to move back to Jetty Beach and take over the Ocean Mark. My ex left me over it. I thought I'd lost my passion and I didn't know how to get it back. But if I'd gone anywhere else, if I'd done anything differently, I wouldn't have been there when you came."

My eyes burn with tears and I bite my lower lip to keep them from spilling.

He takes my hands in his. "This is what it was for. I don't care if you call it fate, or destiny, or blind fucking luck. But I love you more than anything. This is what I want. You. I don't care about anything else. And we're going to have a baby together? God, Sadie, you couldn't have given me *better* news."

I throw my arms around his neck and he nearly picks me up, he hugs me so tight. I'm so overwhelmed, I don't trust myself to speak. This time the tears that trail from the corners of my eyes are tears of joy.

"Don't leave me again, Sadie," he says, his voice soft in my ear. "Let me keep you safe. Let me love you."

"I won't. I promise. But what are we going to do?"

"We'll deal with Adam," he says. "We'll find a way. And we don't have to do it alone."

24

GABE

The lights are dim in Finn's pub. It's late, I just did an unbelievable amount of driving—Sadie was seven hours away, and then I turned around and brought her back—and I can't remember the last time I slept. But none of that matters. I brought my woman home, and she's safe with me now.

I glance over at her table. She's sitting with Emma, Juliet, and Becca. They were here waiting for us when we arrived. I texted Finn and Lucas to keep them updated while I was gone, so they knew what was happening. Hunter has been working on locating Adam. We all met here when we got back into town, and the girls pounced on Sadie as soon as we walked in the door. They had water, tea, snacks—Juliet even brought a fluffy blanket to wrap around her shoulders.

As much as I want to be near her—touching her—it's comforting to see her with friends, caring for her. The way women know how to do for each other. She told them right away about the baby, and I'm glad she did. They all hugged her and congratulated her, telling her how excited they are. Now they have something to talk about that isn't Adam.

We're handling that at our table.

Finn closed the pub early, so we're the only ones in here. He and Lucas sit with me near the bar, empty plates still cluttering the center of the table. Hunter walks out from the kitchen. He got up to take a call a few minutes ago, and the rest of us knew better than to ask questions. I know it has something to do with finding Adam. Hunter's a stand-up guy, but he's a retired Marine turned private security consultant, and I'm discovering he has resources and connections that are... interesting.

"I have eyes on him," Hunter says, pitching his voice low as he takes a seat. The women know what we're talking about, but the four of us want to spare them the details so they won't worry any more than they already are. "He has a room at the Shilo. Driving a Ford pickup with Missouri plates. Didn't do much today. Drove around. Stopped at a store. He never drove near your house. But I can't say whether or not he knows where you live, or where Sadie would be."

"So what do we do?" Finn asks. "Call the police?"

I shake my head. "We don't have anything on him. The fire department is still conducting their investigation, and there's no guarantee they'll find proof. And what he did to Sadie was in another state, and she already dropped those charges. The police won't have a reason to even bring him in for questioning."

"We can't just do nothing," Lucas says. "The guy's a fucking lunatic."

"No, nothing isn't an option," I say. "We need to get rid of this guy."

"What are we talking about here?" Lucas asks. "Like, really getting rid of him?"

"Jesus," Finn says. "This is some serious shit."

"Look, as much as I'd love to get my hands on him and make him regret everything he's done, we can't go vigilante. He's not worth the risk to our families." I look at Hunter. I've thought this through. "We have children to think about."

Hunter nods. "Then we have to work within the law."

"Okay, so how do we do that?" Finn asks.

I rub my chin and stare at the table for a long moment. "We need to do two things. First, we need to make sure the fucker knows if he ever shows his face here again, we *will* end him. I don't want to go to prison, but if he comes back..." I take a deep breath to cool the hot coal of anger that smolders in my gut. "Second, we need the law to get their hands on him. I don't know if Sadie can reopen her case in Missouri, but if we can at least get him to admit to the arson, that will be a start."

"We need a confession," Hunter says.

"So how do we do that?" Lucas asks. "We can't exactly kidnap and waterboard him."

Everyone's eyes dart to Hunter. I think we're all wondering if he knows how to do that.

"We need a way to record him," Hunter says. "Get him talking and have a record of it. But you can't record someone without their consent. It's illegal here."

"What about the security system at my house?" I ask. "If we somehow get him to my place, can we record him there? It has audio, and if I move the cameras, they can record anywhere."

Hunter taps the table a few times. "That gets into shaky legal ground. I have a cop friend I can call and ask, but I think even home security systems fall under wiretapping laws. Especially the audio recordings, which is what we'd need. He'd have to..."

"Have to what?" I ask.

"Break in," Hunter says. "If he breaks into your house, your home security footage would be admissible as evidence. If he confesses to the fire, and even to Sadie's assault in the process..."

"So you're saying we need to get him to break into Gabe's house, and then admit to committing other crimes?" Lucas asks, his voice laced with skepticism. "That sounds impossible."

"Not necessarily," I say. "We'd just need to provoke him enough to do it."

Hunter meets my eyes. "I think you're right. He needs to be unhinged. It will make him more dangerous, but I can be there to make sure nothing goes to shit. The thing is, we're going to need Sadie. She's the only way this will work."

My eyes dart to her. She's smiling at Emma, laughing softly at something one of the girls said. She's terrified of Adam, and if I had my way, she'd never see him again. It's like a kick to the gut, thinking about putting her through this. But I know my Sadie is strong enough. I know she can do it.

I nod, a plan forming in my mind. "If you know where he is, we can put ourselves in his path. Make sure he sees us, get him to follow us back to my place." I take a breath, because this is the riskiest part, and I hate putting her in even the smallest amount of danger. "If I make it look like I've left, he might break in."

Hunter nods along as I talk. "You'll have to provoke him hard-core to make sure he does it. He needs to be angry as hell. Rash."

"I think I know exactly how to do that," I say. I glance at Sadie again. *I'm sorry baby. We'll get through this together.*

"If you can do that, just make sure your security system is up and running," Hunter says. "I'll be at your house in case he shows up armed or something else unexpected happens. If he won't talk, we can at least get him for breaking and entering, and if he's already in custody, the police might get something out of him about the fire."

"He'll talk," I say. "We'll find a way."

"We'll help too," Lucas says. "You guys aren't doing this alone."

"Absolutely," Finn says.

"So how are you going to make sure he sees you?" Lucas asks.

"Same way we're going to make sure we get him enraged enough to follow us home and break into my house," I say. "He's at the Shilo, and there's a restaurant there. We're going to throw an impromptu baby shower for Sadie."

25

SADIE

A low hum of voices fills the air. I'm surrounded by pink and blue helium-filled balloons, a big mylar baby bottle in the middle of them. When Gabriel told us the plan, Emma, Juliet, and Becca sprang into action. Somehow they threw together a convincing baby shower in less than twenty-four hours.

Granted, I'm barely pregnant, and not showing, which makes a baby shower seem odd. But I'm wearing a loose shirt that makes it look like I could be hiding a belly underneath. And with all the decorations, it's obvious what this is.

Juliet is an absolute genius when it comes to party planning. She said she used to just do organizational consulting, but since she moved to Jetty Beach, she started working with Nicole, planning events. She flits around the restaurant, holding a clipboard, checking things off her list. She managed to get two signs that say *Congratulations Sadie and Gabriel* with little teddy bears, rubber ducks, and pacifiers—one for the restaurant where the supposed shower is being held, and one for the lobby, where it's more likely Adam will see it.

I take a deep breath to calm my nerves and soothe my raw stomach. I threw up four times this morning—whether from the pregnancy, or fear for what we're about to do, I couldn't say.

The reality of what we're doing is such a stark contrast to the scene playing out in front of me. Juliet talking to Emma and Becca. They nod along, and Becca goes to talk to one of the restaurant staff. It's not even a real shower, but they're making sure it looks perfect. Nicole and Clover are here, tying more balloons to the chairs around the long table. Clover brought a cake. When Gabriel reminded her it isn't a real baby shower, she just shrugged, rubbed her pregnant belly and said, "But I want cake."

Ryan is at the table, holding his almost two-year-old daughter, Madeline, in his lap. He absently places little kisses on her head while he talks to his brother, Cody. Cody has Emma and Hunter's one-and-a-half-year-old son Sebastian in his arms, and their other son Isaac sits at a table, coloring in a race car coloring book. Hunter isn't here—he's making sure things are ready at Gabriel's house.

All these perfectly nice, perfectly decent people, throwing a fake baby shower, so we can goad the man who raped me into breaking into Gabriel's house and confessing to arson.

Surreal doesn't even begin to cover it.

When Gabriel told me the plan last night, I thought I might vomit. They're using me as bait. They want Adam to see us here, see that I'm pregnant with another man's baby. They're counting on him being angry enough to do something extreme. That he'll come after me immediately.

The thing is, I think they're absolutely right. He's going to come unglued. There's no doubt in my mind that this is going to work—at least to make him angry. He's going to see the balloons and signs in the lobby; there are so many, no one could miss them. He's going to see my name. I'm sure he'll come investigate. He'll have to know if it's me. And then he'll see me here, with Gabriel. Surrounded by people supposedly celebrating my pregnancy.

He's going to lose his mind.

When we're sure he's seen us—Lucas and Finn are loitering in the lobby and they'll be watching him as soon as he appears—we'll leave. We'll make it look like the shower is over and head back to Gabriel's house, hoping that Adam follows.

My hand drifts to my belly, the nausea swirling in my stomach a reminder that the one part of this baby shower that isn't fake is the baby. He or she is growing inside me. Gabriel's baby.

I was astounded by his reaction when I told him I was pregnant. I thought he'd be shocked. Maybe scared, or even angry. But he was none of those things. He was *happy*. And despite the fact that the last couple days have been utter chaos, he *is* happy. He's happier than I've ever seen him. A light shines in his eyes every time he looks at me. A light that wasn't there before.

I wish I felt the same happiness. But I can't see past today. I don't know what's going to happen when Adam sees me. A million things could go wrong. He could barrel into the restaurant and cause a scene. He could follow us to Gabriel's house, but leave again, planning to get to me in a different way. And if things do go to plan, and he does break in, there's no guarantee he'll confess to anything. He was always brilliant at manipulating people. He had my entire family snowed. He puts on that smooth smile, says the right things, and everyone thinks he's the greatest guy on Earth.

Most of all, I don't know what I'm going to do when I see him.

Aside from the glimpse I got of him at the store, I haven't seen him in months. What is it going to be like to face him again? Am I strong enough to handle this?

Gabriel keeps assuring me that I am. He believes it. I can see it in his eyes, feel it in his lips, in his strong hands. He thinks I can do this.

I hope he's right.

Emma comes over and squeezes my arm, her face full of sympathy. "You doing okay, sweetie?"

"I think so."

"You're going to be fine," she says.

"Thanks. I'm just nervous."

"This all looks very convincing," she says. "I guess now we just have to hope he comes through the lobby and sees it?"

I nod. "Yeah, his truck is still in the parking lot and Hunter said he's definitely here."

I was worried about the time it might take. We can't just stand around all day pretending to have a baby shower. But Gabriel knows the restaurant manager, and when he explained the situation, she said we could use the space for as long as we need it. Customers are being seated at the other tables, so the restaurant can keep doing business as usual.

"It's going to work," she says, bringing me in for a hug.

Deep breath. "I hope so. I just want this to be over."

Gabriel catches my eye. He hasn't been far from me since he found me yesterday. He wouldn't even let me drive back; we left my car hours away, but neither of us cared. We needed to be together—needed to stay close. He held my hand for most of the long drive home, lifting it to his lips to kiss it now and then. He smiles at me now, lending me his strength and assurance.

He's the only person in the world who can cut through my fear. He made the nightmares disappear. I sleep soundly next to him, comfortable and safe. The blissful sensation of his body joined with mine erases the visceral memories of Adam violating me. I no longer relive that horrible day over and over in my mind. The way Gabriel makes love to me is rewriting my story, healing the parts of me that were broken. Giving me back what I'd lost.

I can do this.

Gabriel pulls his phone from his pocket and a second later, he's crossed the distance between us. "Finn just saw him."

My heart feels like it's going to beat out of my chest. My hands tremble as he leads me to the head of the table where Adam will be able to see us from the lobby.

Gabriel puts his arm around me and his firm hold steadies me. He looks at his phone again. "He stopped in front of the banner. Lucas says he's heading our direction."

I can't look. My entire body freezes with panic. He's here. He's here and he knows I'm pregnant and he's going to kill me.

Gabriel rubs slow circles across my back. He leans in and places a soft kiss on my forehead. When he speaks, his voice is low and melodic. "I love you, Sadie."

I turn to him and meet his gaze, getting lost in his vivid blues. From the corner of my eye, I see him. Adam, standing near the entrance to the restaurant, staring. My heart pounds, but I focus on Gabriel. On his gorgeous face, his lips turned up in a smile. On his eyes, drinking me in. On the feel of his strong arm around me.

"You're okay," Gabriel says quietly. He keeps rubbing my

back and his eyes flick toward the lobby once. "Don't look. Keep your eyes on me. He's not coming closer."

I take slow breaths and try to stay calm. Gabriel touches my cheek with a gentle hand and leans in. I grip his shirt and pull him closer. His lips come to mine and he takes my mouth in a deep kiss. It's hot and possessive, and completely inappropriate for the middle of a hotel restaurant. But as he kisses me, he eases my fear.

Gabriel's phone dings. He pulls away to check it, keeping one arm around me. "He's still in the lobby, but he moved to where he can watch us without being seen. That's our cue to leave."

We make a show of saying goodbye to everyone. Gabriel keeps my hand in his, our fingers locked. My skin pings with electricity, knowing Adam is watching us. We walk out to Gabriel's car and his phone dings again.

"He's following."

I nod but don't look back. We get in and drive straight to his house. Gabriel's eyes jump to the rear-view mirror repeatedly. He doesn't have to tell me that Adam's behind us. I can tell by the way he grips the steering wheel with one hand, holding mine tight in the other.

We pull into his driveway. Deep breaths. Get out and go to the front door, like nothing is amiss. I can just hear the rumble of an engine up the street. Adam stopped. He's waiting.

Now we see if this crazy plan of ours worked.

Gabriel unlocks the door and we go inside. Hunter peeks out from the hallway.

"How did it go?" he asks.

"He followed us here," Gabriel says. He turns to me. "Okay, I'm going to leave and I'll make sure he sees me go. I won't be gone for more than a few minutes and I'll sneak in through the back. Remember, Hunter is here, and I won't be long. We won't let him hurt you."

I swallow hard and nod. Gabriel hugs me, holding me against him for a long moment, then slips out the front door.

"I'll be down the hall," Hunter says. "But I have to stay out of sight so he doesn't know I'm here. If he comes in, try to get him to talk."

"Okay."

Everything in my body screams at me to get away. I clench and unclench my fists repeatedly and my heart beats wildly. I wish I could find my anger—my rage. It carried me through so many moments when I thought I'd crack. But all I can feel now as I listen to Gabriel's car drive away is terror.

It's only a minute before I hear another car pull up in front of the house. Then, footsteps up to the door. Four loud knocks, each one like a jolt of lightning down my spine.

"Sadie!"

I freeze. Gabriel just left. It will be at least several minutes before he can park the car out of sight and walk back. Even though I know Hunter is here, what if he doesn't come quickly enough? Everything is happening so fast.

"Sadie, kitten, open the door."

Kitten? Hearing that word cuts through the terror and I feel a flicker of anger. It's tiny, just one red cinder, floating like a spark from a bonfire. I cling to it, willing it to grow.

"What... what are you doing here?" I say, still keeping my distance from the door.

"I'm here for you," he says. There's an edge to his voice. "I've been looking for you for months."

"I'm not letting you in."

There's a thump against the door. I think he hit it. "Kitten, you need to come out here."

The spark of anger grows, burning hotter. "I am *not* your kitten."

"Open the door."

"No."

Another thump. "Sadie, you better let me in."

"Or what?"

"Or I'll break down this fucking door."

Deep breath. "No."

"You don't think I will? Do you think I'll let this piece of wood stand between me and what's mine?"

I take slow steps backward. "I'm not letting you in. And I'm not yours."

"Yes you are," he says, louder now. "I'm here to bring you home."

"This is my home," I say.

"It's okay, kitten," he says, like he's trying to sound soothing. "I know you made a mistake. It doesn't matter. I'll forgive you if you just let me in right now."

"Mistake?" I ask, rage pooling in my belly. "The only mistake I ever made was opening the door for you the last time."

"You're mine," he says, and slams his fist against the door. "Open the goddamn door."

"No."

"Sadie."

"I'm not opening the door," I say, my voice gaining strength. I close my eyes and take a deep breath, knowing what I'm about to say is going to set him off. Knowing that's what we need. "I'm not yours, and I never have been. I'm getting married, Adam." A small lie, but it will add weight. "And I'm having his baby. I'm *his*."

Something slams against the door—hard. I think it's his foot. Gabriel locked the doorknob but left the deadbolt open. Two more kicks. Wood splinters and I gasp, backing up into the kitchen as the door flies open.

Adam stalks in, his eyes murderous, nostrils flaring. "You should have let me in."

"Don't come anywhere near me," I say. "You're never touching me again."

"Don't be stupid." He takes a step forward.

"I'm serious, Adam," I say. "I won't let you hurt me again."

"I never hurt you," he says.

"You raped me, you piece of shit," I say.

An awful smile crosses his face. "Are we still calling it that? Come on, kitten."

"No," I say. "You need to admit it. You need to admit what you did to me."

He tilts his head to the side and spreads his arms wide. "Kitten, you belong to me. You have since we were kids. We're soulmates. You were resisting me and I had to teach you a lesson."

"Teach me a lesson?" I ask.

"I needed to leave my mark on you," he says.

"I said no. I said no and you did it anyway."

A spasm of anger crosses his features. "I don't give a fuck what you said. I took what was mine and I'll do it again. I already told you, you belong to me."

"You're insane," I say, backing away. Where is Gabriel? "You had no right to touch me, and you are never, ever doing it again. I am not yours, do you hear me? I don't care how many times you say it, or how many doors you kick in, or how many buildings you burn down."

"You think that was the last of it?" he asks, his voice hard. He walks toward me, purposeful, backing me into the kitchen. "You think I won't do it again? I'll burn down the whole fucking world. That piece of shit thinks he can touch my woman? Fuck that. I'm going to burn his house next, but this time he'll be in it."

He surges forward and I run into something behind me. He leans in, putting his hands on the kitchen counter on either side of me.

"It's a shame I didn't torch his place when he was there," he says. "But I didn't want to risk burning you too. Now? He's a fucking dead man. I'm going to kill him. Slowly. And you're going to watch. Because you need to learn. You need to understand that I will do anything to keep what's mine. I'll kill for you, Sadie. It was a big mistake for you to run away from me. I need to remind you that you belong to me, you sneaky little bitch."

He grabs me by the back of my neck and I gasp. I feel as if I'm drifting out of my own body, watching the scene play out like an invisible bystander.

"Don't fucking touch her."

There's a loud *thunk* and a sickening crunch. Adam's eyes widen and his mouth drops open. With an odd sense of detachment, I look at the butcher knife sticking out of his hand, pinning it to the counter. At the blood welling up around the blade. At Gabriel's hand gripping the handle.

Gabriel grabs me, pulling me away. Adam lets out an agonizing scream. Hunter comes out, holding a handgun. He hands it to Gabriel, who points it straight at Adam.

"Listen to me, you sick son of a bitch," Gabriel says. "If you ever come anywhere near Sadie again, you won't walk away. I will fucking end you."

Adam's eyes dart from Gabriel, to Hunter, to his bleeding hand. His mouth moves, but no sound comes out.

"Maybe I should just end it now," Gabriel says. "Baby, get out of the way."

"No," I say.

Adam's face whips toward me. He's white as a sheet, a sheen of sweat on his forehead. "That's it, kitten."

I take two steps toward Gabriel and hold my hand out, nodding at the gun. "Give it to me."

Gabriel meets my eyes and nods once, then hands me the gun.

The fear in Adam's eyes burns away my terror. Suddenly, I realize he has no more power over me. This sniveling, manipulative, evil piece of shit can't hurt me. He won't hurt me. I won't let him, and neither will Gabriel.

I lift the gun and point it at his head, my hand steady. When I speak, my voice is calm. "I'm not going to kill you. I don't have to. You're going to walk out of here, in handcuffs. And then you're no longer my problem. After this, I won't think of you again."

I pause there, pointing a loaded gun at his head. The last of the color drains from his face and he starts to shake, cringing away from me. I lower the gun and hand it back to Gabriel. He passes it to Hunter, who flicks the safety and tucks it into the back of his pants.

Hunter nods toward the front door. "I think they're here. I already called."

Gabriel takes my hand and leads me out of the kitchen while Hunter goes to the broken front door. Police officers swarm in, shouting orders at Adam. He yells back, almost incoherent. *She's mine. You can't take her from me. I'll kill them both.* They surround him.

Someone tends to his wound, taking out the knife and binding his hand. He tries to resist, but they slam him over the counter and handcuff him. They lead him outside and his head hangs down. Defeated.

The rest of the afternoon goes by in a haze. Gabriel

holding me tight. Sitting on the couch while police officers question me. Someone gets me a glass of water. I tell them everything. How I know Adam. What he did to me back home. How he raped me. Stalked me. Harassed me. Gabriel gives them a copy of his home security footage. They thank us and assure us they'll keep us posted.

People come to check on us. Emma. Clover. Finn and Juliet. Lucas and Becca. Someone brings dinner, but I don't eat much.

When everyone is gone and the house is quiet, Gabriel gently leads me to bed. We strip off our clothes and get between the sheets. I'm utterly exhausted, but there are no more tears. I don't feel like I need to break down while Gabriel comforts me. I'm strong. I'm whole. I settle into his arms, relishing the feel of his skin against mine, and simply rest.

My nightmare is finally over.

26

GABE

$\mathcal{T}$he burned-out restaurant doesn't look any better.

I wander toward the wreckage, taking stock. It's been a week since I was up here last, and all that's changed is that a heavy rain soaked the pile of ashes and blackened wood that was once my restaurant.

The sound of the waves carries up from the beach below. Without the building, the view is unobstructed, the ocean stretching out as far as the eye can see. A few seagulls circle in the air and a cool breeze blows in from the water. The tide is out, exposing a long expanse of sand.

I bring out my phone and read over the email I got from the police department. I read it once this morning when it arrived. Sadie got a copy too, and neither of us said much about it. We didn't need to.

Adam was arrested for breaking and entering the day we baited him. After the police showed him the footage from my security system, he confessed to the arson. He wouldn't admit he raped Sadie, not in so many words. But the way he described the assault made it clear she had repeatedly said no.

In the truck of his car, they found gasoline, rope, duct tape, several tarps, and a set of knives and razor blades. When they contacted the police department in Missouri, they discovered he matches the description of a man wanted in the cases of a string of rapes across three counties. And his fingerprints are a match for prints found at the scene of several other crimes.

It seems Adam Cooper wasn't just terrorizing Sadie. He's an unstable lunatic who's responsible for so many crimes he's going to prison for a long, long time.

Sadie took the news well. It made her sick to her stomach to think about what they found in his trunk. But something has changed in her since the day he was arrested. She got her power back. She says it's because of me— because of the way I've cared for her. But I don't think so. Maybe I helped her, but this is her strength shining through. She confronted the devil and found him lacking.

I know she'll always carry the scars of what's happened, but I'll be there for her when she struggles. Together, we can move on.

Her hand slips into mine and she leans her head on my arm. "The view is beautiful."

"Yeah, it really is." I squeeze her hand.

I have a decision to make. Where do I go from here? What is my life going to look like in the future?

I could walk away. I could decide this restaurant took too much out of me. Do something else with my life. I try to envision what that life would be like. A life without cooking. Is it time for a new dream?

"It's going to be amazing," Sadie says.

I look at her. "What's going to be amazing?"

"The new restaurant."

I blink at her a few times. "What?"

"Can't you picture it?" she asks. "The old building was nice, but the dining room was too small. And the ceilings could have been taller." She takes a few steps forward, her boots crunching on debris. "I'm imagining a big stone fireplace in the lobby. The windows were perfect, so we won't need to change that. And I've been thinking about a balcony. Can you imagine, outdoor dining on the side of this bluff, overlooking the ocean? It would be amazing during the summer months, and we could put in those outdoor heaters for when it's chilly. You once said you wished it had a private dining room, for small events. We could add that to the design. And that corner in the kitchen you hated? Redesign it. You can have more freezer space. And the wine cellar. Oh my god, Gabriel, you could redesign the wine room completely. Maybe get your contact at the winery to help."

I stare at her. "You've been thinking about this?"

She smiles. "Of course, why wouldn't I be?"

"I don't know, I just..." My throat tightens and I swallow hard. "You seem like you're excited about rebuilding."

"I'm *so* excited," she says, her eyes sparkling. "I have so many ideas. I know I'm not an expert or anything, and we'll have to work with an architect to see what's possible within the budget. I don't know how much leeway we'll have with the design. But I think we can make it incredible. Even better than it was before."

We can make it incredible. We.

I don't know how to articulate what I'm feeling, so I just stand here, staring at her.

When I bought the Ocean Mark, it was the beginning of the end of my marriage. I don't regret that. Amanda wasn't right for me, and it's better that she left, regardless of what I do with my career. Even before I met Sadie, I knew that.

And going through that difficult time meant I was ready for Sadie when we did meet.

I didn't realize until this moment how afraid I was to move forward with rebuilding. To commit to making this happen. Would it be what Sadie wants? Would it be what I want if she didn't?

She does want this. Not only does she want it for me, she wants it for *us*.

I'm so choked with emotion, all I can do is grab her and pull her into me. I hold her tight, stroking her soft hair, breathing her in.

"Are you okay?" she asks.

"Yeah," I say and swallow hard. "I just love you so much."

Her hands thread around my waist and she hugs me back, resting her head against my chest. "I love you, too."

Although I'm standing in front of a ruined dream, it's not ruined at all. It's going to take time and a lot of hard work to get there, but Sadie and I are going to build this dream together. A new one, meant for the two of us.

No, not the two of us. The *three* of us.

From the outside looking in, it might appear as if I had everything taken from me when my restaurant burned down. But I have everything I've ever wanted—everything I've ever needed. My life is complete.

Almost...

27

SADIE

*T*he light fixture tilts in the back seat as I turn the corner. I wince and slow down. It was a floor model, so it's not packed well—just sitting in an open box with a little bit of tissue paper stuffed around the outside for padding. I found it at a shop in town. As soon as I saw it, I knew it would be perfect for the new restaurant. I brought it home to see what Gabriel thinks.

Home. Our home.

I never moved back into my house. There was no question that I would move in with Gabriel. It's no longer out of fear. We wanted to bring our lives together. He said he didn't want to be away from me, and the baby. And I don't want to be away from him either.

Construction on the new restaurant is underway and we've been busy with an endless stream of meetings with the architect, general contractor, engineers, and designers. The new plans are positively stunning. Gabriel was able to put everything he wants into the design—more space, a better layout, tall ceilings, and even a balcony. He's been on site all day, as far as I know. I'm hoping he's home now.

His car is in the driveway when I pull up. I get out of the car, my baby belly only just starting to make it awkward, and grab the light fixture from the back. It's a little unwieldy, but not too heavy. I close the car door with my hip and head inside.

There's noise coming from the kitchen when I come in.

"Hey." I set the box down near the door. "What are you up to in there?"

"Wait there," Gabriel says. "Don't come in yet."

I hesitate near the door, but that's harder than it sounds. Whatever he's cooking smells amazing. My mouth waters and my tummy rumbles. One thing I will say for dating a chef, you never go hungry. In fact, I've spent the last several months eating some of the best food I've ever tasted. Gabriel has been on a creative spree, testing things for the new menu. I'm the lucky one who gets to sample all his new creations.

"Okay, I'm waiting, but I have something to show you."

The baby shifts, a soft fluttery feeling, almost like bubbles. He or she is still so small, but I'm feeling more movement every day. We haven't found out if it's a boy or a girl, but we have an ultrasound scheduled soon. I'm so excited to get a peek at our little one.

The fact that Gabriel and I are having a baby together is still a little bit surreal. I find myself rubbing my belly, grateful for the reminder that this is all actually happening. This child. This man. This life.

It's more than I ever could have hoped for.

After Adam was arrested, I sent my parents a copy of the footage from the security system. By their replies, they were stunned, and horrified. They begged me to forgive them and come back home. Even my brother sent a long message to apologize.

I've done one of those things. I did forgive them. But I didn't do it for *them*. I did it for me, so I could move on.

I'm slowly letting them know more about my life, but although I can forgive, I'll never really trust them. I discussed it with both Gabriel and my therapist, and they agreed that it's healthy for me to allow the rift with my family to heal, while still keeping them at a safe distance.

Forgiveness has given me peace. I'm not angry at them anymore, and that's a beautiful thing.

Gabriel comes out of the kitchen wearing an apron that says *Hot Stuff Coming Through*. I bought it for him as a joke, but he wears it all the time at home.

"What are you up to in there?" I ask.

He kisses me, his hand lingering on my belly. "You'll see."

"Whatever you're cooking in there better be for me," I say. "I'm starving."

"You know I love to feed my woman," he says, placing a little kiss on my nose.

"Good, but here, look." I point to the light fixture.

He grabs it by the top and carefully picks it up. "This is beautiful."

"I was thinking it would go really well in that alcove by the private dining room."

"I agree, it's perfect." He sets it carefully back in the box. "Okay, my turn."

He leads me into the dining room. The table is set for two, complete with a crisp white tablecloth and candles in the center. He pulls out a chair and I sit down.

I take the cloth napkin and place it in my lap while he brings out two plated meals.

"It's pan seared scallops, wrapped in bacon, with an

herbed parmesan risotto," he says, sliding one plate carefully in front of me.

I breathe in the aroma—savory bacon, a hint of garlic,
fresh herbs. "I like it already."

He smiles, but doesn't sit down. Sometimes he sits with
me and eats, but other times he just wants to know what I
think.

My fork slides through one of the scallops and I bring
the bite to my mouth. My tongue pushes the food as I chew.
I like to really concentrate on my first bite. Closing my eyes,
I let the flavors settle. The bit of bacon is deliciously crisp
and a tiny bit salty, which complements the warm, tender
scallop perfectly. It's so good I almost moan. He's such a
genius.

"This is ama—"

My eyes open and I stop. Gabriel is no longer standing
next to the table, waiting for me to tell him what I think.
He's kneeling next to me.

On one knee.

He takes my hand and I don't know if there's a cascade of
butterflies in my tummy, or if the baby just did a somersault.

"Sadie, I knew a long time ago that I wanted to marry
you. Do you remember the day we went out of town? When
you came to the restaurant to talk me into going away with
you for a couple days?"

I nod. I don't trust myself to speak.

"I knew then," he says. "I typed *love you* when we were
texting, and I deleted it because I hadn't told you yet. But I
knew. It wasn't just that I loved you. People say that all the
time, and they even mean it. But they aren't necessarily
ready for what I'm about to ask you. I was ready. I was ready
that day to commit to you forever, and I've been waiting for
the right time to do this ever since."

He produces a small black velvet box, but just holds it. "We've been through a lot and I'll always be so grateful that you came into my life. I know you think I helped you, but Sadie, you saved me. I was so lost before you. I was lonely and sad. I was grumpy all the time because it seemed like all around me were people living perfect, happy lives. And then there you were, looking at me with those dazzling green eyes, and everything changed. I'd lost my way, and you helped me find my purpose again. Find my passion. You gave me a reason—a reason for everything."

With a deep breath, he opens the box. A ring sparkles, the candlelight flickering off the diamond.

"Oh, Gabriel," I breathe.

"Sadie, will you be my wife?"

"Yes," I say, before the words are even out of his mouth.

Gabriel smiles—that smile that I love so much, that's not a secret anymore—and takes out the ring. I hold up my hand, trying not to tremble, and he slides it onto my finger.

He touches my face and brings his lips to mine. I wrap my arms around his shoulders, melting into his kiss.

When he pulls back, he smiles, his eyes sparkling. "I love you."

"I love you, too. So much."

"You're still thinking about the food, aren't you?" he asks.

I laugh. "Is that bad? I'm starving."

He brings my hand to his lips and kisses my fingers. "Of course not. Let's eat."

EPILOGUE

GABE

ne year later...

"AND THIS IS DADDY'S FAVORITE." I pinch a little bit of chocolate mousse between my fingers and bring it up to Violet's mouth.

"Gabriel?" Sadie peeks her head through the doorway. "What are you doing back here? You're not trying to help, are you?"

"No." I kiss the top of Violet's head. "Just showing my little cupcake a few things."

"Don't sneak her any food," she says with a smile.

"I know, I know." I look down at my daughter and quickly wipe the smudge of mousse from the corner of her tiny mouth. I'm holding her facing outward, propped on one arm, my other hand holding her tummy to keep her steady. Her face turns up to mine and her big green eyes sparkle as her mouth opens in a gummy smile. "You don't have any teeth, do you cupcake?"

I tickle her and she squirms, letting out a soft giggle.

"Don't hide back here too long," Sadie says. "People are starting to arrive."

"I won't." I smile at my wife.

My wife. It's amazing how much I love the way that sounds. Sadie Parker. Our wedding was small, just a few close friends and family. Sadie wanted to get married before Vi was born, and I couldn't wait to marry her, so it all worked out. I'll never forget how beautiful she looked that day.

Of course, she's beautiful every day.

I step out of the way of Marcus, the new assistant chef. He's handling the food for the event today, since I'm supposed to be a guest.

"I guess we should see who's here," I say, adjusting my grip on Violet. She kicks her legs as I smooth down her little pink dress. The little bit of hair she has—red just like her mommy's—is held in a tiny clip. At six months old, she's not very mobile, but she likes to be able to look around and see what's going on.

The new restaurant has been up and running for months, but sometimes I still look around in awe. The building turned out better than I could have hoped. It's stunning. Tall ceilings and huge windows make it feel spacious and airy, while the soft lighting enhances the intimacy of the dining room. The décor is elegant, while still retaining a local flavor.

We kept some features of the original building, like the exposed wood beams and a large stone fireplace in the lobby. The kitchen itself is a dream. Being able to design it from scratch meant I could have everything to my exact preferences and specifications. The first night I cooked here felt like coming home. There was no period of adjustment, or figuring out a new routine. It was perfect.

It's too cold to use the outdoor dining space on the balcony, and the new private dining room is too small, so the baby shower is being held in the main part of the restaurant. Sadie and Emma are setting out the last of the centerpieces—each table gets a vase with a spray of pink, blue, and yellow flowers. Off to the side are two empty tables for gifts, decorated with balloons and a little banner that says, *Congratulations!* strung between them. The restaurant staff is busy setting out brunch. Violet wiggles her feet again as we pass by the food.

"It smells good, doesn't it?" I bounce her a little. "Don't worry, cupcake. Daddy will get you a bite when Mommy isn't looking."

"Hey Gabe?" Emma says. "Do you see Hunter anywhere?"

I move to where I can see out into the lobby. Hunter is lying on the floor, bench pressing their two-year old son Sebastian while his big brother Isaac laughs. "He's out front, messing around with Sebby."

"Is Isaac with them?"

"Yep. Do you want me to get them for you?"

"No, that's okay." She adjusts the flowers in one of the centerpieces. "Just want to make sure my boys are all accounted for."

The front door opens and Jackson holds the door for his wife, Melissa. He has their younger daughter Leah in his arms—she's around a year old—and their older daughter Skylar comes in holding Melissa's hand. Behind them are Ryan and Nicole—Ryan holding Madeline, and Nicole has their brand new baby Amelia in her arms.

I shake hands with Jackson and hug Melissa when they

come through to the dining room. "Good to see you. It's been a while."

"I still can't get over how great this place looks," Melissa says.

"Thanks," I say.

Jackson shifts Leah to his other arm. "I'll be in town for the next week or so. We should talk."

Melissa looks up at him with her eyebrows raised. "Talk about what?"

"Building a resort on the adjacent property," he says.

"Always looking for the next deal," she says.

"I see an opportunity," he says. "I'm still interested, and I know a few others who might be as well."

"Sounds good," I say. A resort next door would be huge for the restaurant. Jackson brought it up last time we were all at the Jacobsen's for dinner, and I've been kicking around some ideas since then. I wouldn't want to run it, but if we found the right people, it could work. It's good to hear he's still interested. Having a man like Jackson Bennett as a potential investor could make this possible.

"Mommy?" Skylar tugs on Melissa's arm. "Is Miss Becca here yet?"

"I don't see her yet," Melissa says. "But I see Isaac over there. Do you want to go play?"

Skylar nods.

"Okay, but don't run," Melissa says.

"Sky, can I come?" Madeline says. She dive bombs out of Ryan's arms. Skylar takes her hand and leads her toward a table set up with craft supplies for the kids.

Sadie comes over, smiling at Nicole, and looks down at the baby in her arms. "Look at her. She's getting so big already."

"I know, they change so fast," Nicole says, glancing down at Amelia.

"My turn," Ryan says, carefully scooping his baby daughter into his arms. "There's my girl."

"I better go make sure there aren't scissors over there," Nicole says, glancing toward the craft table. "Madeline might try to cut Skylar's hair again."

More guests arrive. Friends of Juliet and Becca. Finn's mom. Lucas's father. They set their gifts on the table and people start sampling from the buffet.

Cody and Clover come in with their toddler, Chase.

"Gabe, look!" Clover says. She sets Chase on his feet and he wobbles a little. Then he seems to find his balance and takes a few halting steps forward, his curly blond hair bouncing when he abruptly sits. "He just started doing it this morning."

"He's starting to walk already?" I ask. Violet kicks her legs again and smiles down at Chase. "Vi, your friend Chase is walking. What do you think about that?"

Violet answers by drooling on my hand.

Finally, the guests of honor arrive. Lucas holds the door open for Becca. She's wearing a yellow dress with a white sweater, her pregnant belly sticking straight out in front of her. Juliet isn't far behind, in a blue sweater and dark pants, looking just as pregnant as Becca. Their babies are due within a month of each other, so Sadie decided to throw them a joint baby shower.

More people arrive, and the gifts pile up. The hum of conversation grows as the restaurant fills. The food is a hit, the couples open their presents. I pass Vi to Sadie for a while so she can feed her.

I step back into the doorway of the kitchen and watch. My friends, my family, all here in my restaurant. My two best friends becoming fathers. An ever-increasing bunch of kids, all growing up together. My wife, holding our daughter, a smile on her face.

I can't imagine anything better.

After a couple of hours, the party winds down and people start heading home. The toddlers of the group are tired. Violet is fast asleep in Sadie's arms. She's standing with Juliet and Becca, the three of them talking and laughing softly.

I find Finn and Lucas outside on the balcony, standing by the railing near one of the propane heaters. The beach stretches out below, the waves crashing against the wide expanse of sand.

"How are you two doing?" I ask.

Finn takes a breath. "I don't know, man. I'm getting a little nervous."

"Don't worry," I say. "As soon as you see that baby, it all comes together. I don't know how to describe it. When Violet was born, it was like the world stopped turning for a minute. She was so tiny and perfect. I fell in love with her instantly."

"I will say, you're a different guy since Sadie," Finn says. "Even more so since Violet was born."

"No more grumpy chef," Lucas says.

I shake my head because I know they're right. "What about you?" I ask Lucas.

"I'm awesome," he says, his tone matter-of-fact.

"You're not even nervous about having a baby, are you?" Finn asks.

Lucas shrugs. "Not really. Becca's basically the child whisperer. I won't be able to screw up our kid too much with her as a mom." He glances inside to where Becca, Juliet, and Sadie are chatting near the window and a smile crosses his face. "Besides, look at her. She's fucking adorable. She said let's try for a baby and I was like, you don't need to ask me twice. What my darling wants, my darling gets."

"It's crazy, isn't it?" Finn asks. "Us three, married, having kids."

I look at the three women standing in the window. Sadie holds Violet with her head on her shoulder. She sways back and forth while she talks, gently stroking our daughter's back. Juliet laughs, her smile bright. Becca's eyebrows lift and her hand darts to her belly. She says something and Juliet and Sadie both reach out to touch where she tells them. Feeling the baby move.

I glance over at Finn and Lucas. They're watching our wives, looks of wonder on their faces. I know exactly how they feel.

"You guys are going to be fine." I clap Finn on the back. "Just remember the magic words."

"What's that?" Lucas asks.

"I'll take the baby for a while; you go take a nap."

"Good advice," Finn says. "Thanks for this, by the way. Juliet's really happy."

"Yeah, thanks," Lucas says. "I wasn't so sure about the couples' baby shower thing, but this was good."

"No problem," I say. "We were happy to do it. And it's good to have this place running smoothly."

When everyone is gone, including the guests of honor and their piles of gifts, I take my girls home. Violet is fussy after the long day, so I take her after she's fed and rock her until her eyes get heavy. With great care, I lay her down in her crib, then tiptoe out silently so as not to wake her.

Sadie is in the bedroom, so I head into the kitchen and pour us each a glass of wine. While I'm standing at the counter, she sidles up next to me, wrapping her arms around my waist.

"She asleep?" she asks.

"Yeah," I say. "I rocked her for a while. I think she was a little overstimulated from the party today."

"I bet. Thanks for getting her to bed."

"Of course," I say. "I don't get to do it often enough."

"What are you thinking about?" she asks. "You've been quiet today."

I pause for a moment, considering. "It's just amazing how much has changed over the last few years. There were so many kids there today, you know? I wonder what it will be like a year or two from now. Emma and Hunter want another baby. I bet Cody and Clover will too." I take a deep breath and pull her closer. "I was thinking how grateful I am that I have you, and we have Violet. I'm not missing out on this life."

"I'm grateful too," she says.

"Maybe we should have made the restaurant bigger," I say. "If people keep having kids, we aren't going to be able to fit all of them when someone wants to throw a party."

She laughs. "True. Especially because…"

"Because what?" I ask, leaning away so I can look at her.

She meets my eyes. "Because we're going to add one more."

I lift my eyebrows. "Are you?"

She nods. "I'm pregnant again. We're going to have another baby."

I smile and kiss her forehead. "I know."

"What?" she asks, drawing back. "How did you know? I just found out today."

"I could just tell. I looked at you a few days ago, and I could see it. I've been waiting to see if I was right." I lean in and put my face in her neck, taking a deep breath. "Plus, you smell different when you're pregnant."

She laughs. "Do I? So what do you think, will it be a boy or another little girl?"

"That I don't know," I say. "But I'll be happy either way."

I draw her against me and rest my cheek against her head. My wife. My Sadie.

My life began when we met. I think in some ways, hers did too. Despite the roads we each had to take to find each other, it was worth it. In me, she found a reason to trust again. In her, I found a reason to care.

In her, I found a reason to love.

AUTHOR'S NOTE

The Path to You deals with the very difficult topic of sexual assault.

According to RAINN (Rape, Abuse & Incest National Network), every 98 seconds an American is sexually assaulted. On average, there are 321,500 victims (age 12 and older) of rape and sexual assault in the United States each year.

If you are the victim of sexual assault, you are not alone. And it is not your fault.

Please reach out for help if you've been sexually assaulted. Tell someone you trust. Go to the authorities. Or call the National Sexual Assault Hotline (in the US) at 800-656-HOPE or online at hotline.rainn.org. It's free, anonymous, and confidential. In the UK, you can visit Victim Support at www.victimsupport.org.uk. There are also numerous other national and local organizations and support systems that can help.

AFTERWARD

Dear reader,

Where do I even begin?

I introduced Gabriel Parker way back in Cody and Clover's story. He meets Clover, samples her cooking, and ultimately offers her a job. We see him again in book four (Hunter and Emma's story). He's Emma's older brother, and offers her a place to stay while she gets back on her feet.

I'd always intended for Gabe to be a hero in a Jetty Beach romance. How could I not give this guy his HEA? In fact, I started a book about him right after I finished book four. Let me just say, it's better that I stopped. The story wasn't right, and I knew it. Gabe needed something special, and that wasn't it.

When I started planning the next Jetty Beach book, my intent was to begin with Gabe. After all, Jetty Beach fans already knew him. You'd been bugging me to write his story for a while. It made sense to begin with him and segue into the other two heroes in the series.

But Finn had other plans, and let's be honest, how could I deny Finn anything?

So it took me a little longer to get to Gabe than originally anticipated, so I knew he would need to be worth the wait.

When we begin the book, Gabe has become the odd guy out. He knows everyone in Jetty Beach; in one way or another, he's connected to all the previous couples. So he's been through all the weddings, watched his friends and loved ones have babies, and he's the last remaining single guy of the bunch. And he's not particularly happy about that. He's not man whoring his way around town, living up his post-shitty-marriage existence. He's pouring himself into his work, and his personal life leaves a lot to be desired.

Sadie begins in a very different place. She's suffered a devastating sexual assault at the hands of someone close to her family—her brother's childhood best friend. She chose to cut ties with her family and move where she hopes her abuser won't find her.

She is struggling with the effects of the trauma, and working very hard to begin a new life. But moving on from such a devastating experience isn't easy.

But who better to gently help her through that than Gabriel Parker.

I joked to a friend once or twice that Gabe is a literal angel—and I didn't even make the connection to his name at first. He's patient, loving, gentle, and protective of the woman he loves. Once he understands the full truth of what Sadie went through, he's willing to do anything for her. Anything to make her happy and whole again.

If you've been reading the Jetty Beach books, or any CK novels, you know I have a soft spot for good men. I don't try to make my characters perfect (that would be boring), so they are flawed. But we're all flawed, and even an imperfect person can be a good one. And Gabs is a good man, through and through.

I admired Sadie's strength in making hard choices. She was intensely vulnerable, especially in some of her more poignant moments with Gabe, but through it all, she was a survivor. Through Sadie, it was my intention to treat the issue of sexual assault with respect. The choices I made with regard to her character, her reactions and responses, and the way her physical relationship with Gabe unfolded, were designed to acknowledge the reality of what a sexual assault victim must live through—because the trauma doesn't end when the assault is over.

I hope you enjoyed Gabe and Sadie's story. It's been an absolute pleasure to write these Jetty Beach romances. It's possible this is the last. But I don't like to talk in absolutes. You never know what the future holds.

Thanks for reading,

CK

ALSO BY CLAIRE KINGSLEY

For a full and up-to-date listing of Claire Kingsley books visit
www.clairekingsleybooks.com/books/

For comprehensive reading order, visit www.
clairekingsleybooks.com/reading-order/

The Haven Brothers

Small-town romantic suspense with CK's signature endearing
characters and heartwarming happily ever afters. Can be read as
stand-alones.

Obsession Falls (Josiah and Audrey)

Storms and Secrets (Zachary and Marigold)

The rest of the Haven brothers will be getting their own happily
ever afters!

How the Grump Saved Christmas (Elias and Isabelle)

A stand-alone, small-town Christmas romance.

The Bailey Brothers

Steamy, small-town family series with a dash of suspense. Five
unruly brothers. Epic pranks. A quirky, feuding town. Big HEAs.
Best read in order.

Protecting You (Asher and Grace part 1)

Fighting for Us (Asher and Grace part 2)

Unraveling Him (Evan and Fiona)

Rushing In (Gavin and Skylar)

Chasing Her Fire (Logan and Cara)

Rewriting the Stars (Levi and Annika)

The Miles Family

Sexy, sweet, funny, and heartfelt family series with a dash of
suspense. Messy family. Epic bromance. Super romantic. Best read
in order.

Broken Miles (Roland and Zoe)

Forbidden Miles (Brynn and Chase)

Reckless Miles (Cooper and Amelia)

Hidden Miles (Leo and Hannah)

Gaining Miles: A Miles Family Novella (Ben and Shannon)

Dirty Martini Running Club

Sexy, fun, feel-good romantic comedies with huge... hearts. Can be
read as stand-alones.

Everly Dalton's Dating Disasters (Prequel with Everly, Hazel, and
Nora)

Faking Ms. Right (Everly and Shepherd)

Falling for My Enemy (Hazel and Corban)

Marrying Mr. Wrong (Sophie and Cox)

Flirting with Forever (Nora and Dex)

~

Bluewater Billionaires

Hot romantic comedies. Lady billionaire BFFs and the badass heroes who love them. Can be read as stand-alones.

The Mogul and the Muscle (Cameron and Jude)

The Price of Scandal, Wild Open Hearts, and Crazy for Loving You

More Bluewater Billionaire shared-world romantic comedies by Lucy Score, Kathryn Nolan, and Pippa Grant

~

Bootleg Springs

by Claire Kingsley and Lucy Score

Hot and hilarious small-town romcom series with a dash of mystery and suspense. Best read in order.

Whiskey Chaser (Scarlett and Devlin)

Sidecar Crush (Jameson and Leah Mae)

Moonshine Kiss (Bowie and Cassidy)

Bourbon Bliss (June and George)

Gin Fling (Jonah and Shelby)

Highball Rush (Gibson and I can't tell you)

~

Book Boyfriends

Hot romcoms that will make you laugh and make you swoon. Can be read as stand-alones.

Book Boyfriend (Alex and Mia)

Cocky Roommate (Weston and Kendra)

Hot Single Dad (Caleb and Linnea)

Finding Ivy (William and Ivy)

A unique contemporary romance with a hint of mystery. Stand-alone.

His Heart (Sebastian and Brooke)

A poignant and emotionally intense story about grief, loss, and the transcendent power of love. Stand-alone.

The Always Series

Smoking hot, dirty talking bad boys with some angsty intensity. Can be read as stand-alones.

Always Have (Braxton and Kylie)

Always Will (Selene and Ronan)

Always Ever After (Braxton and Kylie)

The Jetty Beach Series

Sexy small-town romance series with swoony heroes, romantic HEAs, and lots of big feels. Can be read as stand-alones.

Behind His Eyes (Ryan and Nicole)

One Crazy Week (Melissa and Jackson)

Messy Perfect Love (Cody and Clover)

ABOUT THE AUTHOR

Claire Kingsley is a #1 Amazon bestselling author of sexy, heartfelt contemporary romance and romantic comedies. She writes sassy, quirky heroines, swoony heroes who love their women hard, panty-melting sexytimes, romantic happily ever afters, and all the big feels.

She can't imagine life without coffee, her Kindle, and the sexy heroes who inhabit her imagination. She lives in the inland Pacific Northwest with her three kids.

www.clairekingsleybooks.com